Peter Dickinson was born in Zamb[...]
Cambridge. Afterwards he worked a[...]
including reviewing detective novels. His own first two crime
novels, *Skin Deep* (U.S. title, *The Glass-Sided Ants' Nest*) and *A
Pride of Heroes* (*The Old English Peep Show*), set an unsurpassed
record by winning the Crime Writers' Gold Dagger Award in
successive years. He has also become an important writer for
young adults, winning the Guardian award for *The Blue Hawk*, the
Carnegie Medal and Whitbread Award for *Tulka* and the Carnegie
Medal for *City of Gold*.

Of his own work, Peter Dickinson writes, "I'm like a
beachcomber walking along the shores of my imagination, picking up things and wondering what kinds of structures they could
make."

PETER DICKINSON

NOVELS

The Glass-Sided Ants' Nest (Skin Deep)*
The Old English Peep Show (A Pride of Heros)
The Sinful Stones (The Seals)
Sleep and His Brother
The Lizard in the Cup
The Green Gene
The Poison Oracle
The Lively Dead
King and Joker
Walking Dead
One Foot in the Grave
The Last Houseparty
Hindsight
Death of a Unicorn
Tefuga
Perfect Gallows*
Skeleton In Waiting

* available from the Library of Crime Classics ®

PETER DICKINSON

The Glass-Sided Ants' Nest

LIBRARY OF CRIME CLASSICS®

MISTER E'S™

INTERNATIONAL POLYGONICS, LTD.
NEW YORK CITY

The characters in this book are entirely imaginary and bear no relation to any living characters.

THE GLASS-SIDED ANTS' NEST

Library of Congress Card Catalog No. 91-70596
ISBN 1-55882-089-2

Printed and manufactured in the United States of America.
First IPL printing July, 1991.
10 9 8 7 6 5 4 3 2 1

1

"Slower, please."

Impassively the driver slipped into third and the car began to dawdle down the wide street.

Too impassively? James Pibble stared at the cropped and disciplined neck, wondering how the gossip ran about him in the lower reaches of the Yard. Lives ago, he'd been a sprat in those waters himself, and then he and all the other sprats had evolved a shared mythology about the big fish—this one a lecher, this one a miracle-worker, this one a near villain—and mostly they'd been right. What did the current generation of sprats make of Superintendent Pibble, aging, unglamorous, graying toward retirement? Did they know how much luck had gone into his reputation for having a knack with kooky cases? Probably. And did they know about the Adversary?

Wandering unwary through the jungle of self, Pibble fell into the pit. Normally he'd have had Sergeant Crewe with him, but Asian flu was sifting the Yard, and two men couldn't be spared where one would do, so now he wallowed in the dread which haunted all new beginnings. To what did it go back? Some party for tots at which a bigger tot had smiled him to scorn? Had he come from the womb haunted? Not every new case, not every supper party in a strange house, produced its Adversary, the lounging, contemptuous male who shriveled his soul. Pibble had, in his time, sent Adversaries to prison—Walewski, for instance—but that didn't exorcise them. This time, perhaps . . .

Defensively, as if to study the ambience of murder, he leaned forward and peered at the tidy terraces: a red door, a turquoise door, a brown door picked out in white, a tangerine door picked out in black—the district had swallowed a lot of money and paint since he was last down this way. Crippen, wasn't that an antique shop? What used to be there, a tobacconist? And the fish-and-chip shop was gone—and the vet, too. The doors had brass dolphins for knockers and upper-middle-class prams stood on the pavement, each with its tiny Dominic or Miranda or Camilla or Adam resting in the dusty May sunshine. Prams are a dead giveaway; if the same tribes had still been living here as did when Pibble used to come down, fifteen years back, to rouse small-time burglars out of bed (three families to a house then, gas cookers on each landing, one cold tap, outside lav, the odor of damp dirt), there'd have been prams all right, but different. Shiny, streamlined, jazzy with chrome—not these staid barouches.

Well, well, all London was changing, changing, dreadfully changing. Estate agents must be doing nicely down this way, with a constant flow of moneyed youngsters moving in with one kid and moving out with three. Pretty it all looked, with the easy, plain proportions shown off by the fresh paint. Rum sort of area for a black man to get his head bashed in. The car swung north.

Wrong again. Just the sort of area for a black man to get his head bashed in. Flagg Terrace hadn't changed by so much as a dirty dishcloth drying at a window. The tide of money had washed around it. The hordes of conquering young executives, sweeping down like Visigoths from the east and driving the cowering and sullen aboriginals into the remoter slums of Acton, had left it alone. Neither taste nor wealth could assail its inherent dreadfulness. Pibble suddenly realized that he had never kept a promise to himself, made full fifteen years back, that he would look up Flagg and find out something about the man who had designed and built this thing.

It was like a late, phony Tudor castle turned inside out, a crenelated cul-de-sac. The bricks were an implacable and unweathered bull's-blood, picked out in ruglike patterns with other blue-black bricks. To counterpoint these aimless crisscrosses, the plumbers had imposed their own pattern of vigorous verticals and horizontals—drainpipes and vent pipes and rising mains and rain-water pipes—with profuse virtuosity down every façade. Stone steps ran up to the front doors; under each flight of steps was a dark arch, full of ungarnered milk empties; above each a lowering porch, crenelated but without the expected portcullis. There were twelve such houses in the cul-de-sac. A uniformed policeman—a rather little one with a blond beard—stood at the door of No. 9, halfway down the western side, and a few bored loungers watched him. No photographers, Pibble observed; except when Fleet Street has one of its fits of liberalism, black men don't rate much press coverage, even with their heads bashed in. He wondered why Sandy Graham had sent so smartly for the Yard. Something a little unusual there.

"Unusual? No, Jimmy. We've got a lovely little setup here, really airy-fairy. Just the thing for Pibble, I said, the moment I'd seen the Kus."

"Coos?"

"Every single member of the household, me dear, is called Ku. They're a tribe from New Guinea somewhere. Deceased's a Ku, suspects all Kus, witnesses all Kus, only there aren't any witnesses." Superintendent Graham vented his strange contralto giggle.

"Any of them speak English?"

"Oh Lord, yes, according to their lights. Then there's **Dr.**

Ku. She's as white as I am. Or you," Graham added grudgingly. "She's English."

"British," corrected the silent figure in the gloom behind Graham's left elbow.

Graham swung his hulk around toward the voice with the ponderous dignity of a swing bridge. "Sergeant Pauncefort, may I beg you in future to leave the susceptibilities of Celtic minorities to my care?"

Jesus, thought Pibble, I'm not going to get much help from Sandy if he's starting his cross-talk bit with Pauncy this soon. He's got something to hide—this must be a real sticky one. Why's he got it in for me now? He used to be an honest copper under that gloating hulk. Ah, who can one trust?

"Jimmy boy," said Graham, turning back to him, "this is going to be a sticky one. You'll find out why. And I'm up to my virginal eyebrows and can't be much use to you. But I do think it's your cup of tea, honest. Come and have a squint at the deader and you'll see what I mean. Never seen anything like it. I blew my top at first, but then I thought there wasn't much point in having him moved back and provoking a race riot or something. There's plenty of blood on the stairs to show where the poor bastard bought it—all that's clear enough. Then I'll introduce you to Dr. Ku and leave you to get on with it."

The stairwell was not as brightly lit as the Borough Council would have wished. There was a 25-watt bulb in the big hallway and another on the first landing, but the chocolate-and-beige lincrusta walls seemed to suck in their yellow light, leaving a jungly gloom which smelled much less dirty than Pibble had expected. Luckily there was a window at the half landing, a stained-glass rendering of "Love Locked Out." The heavy leading employed by the craftsmen lent a peculiar emphasis to the anatomy of the naked figure leaning on the doorpost, but this unfortunate accent was compensated for by the amount of light let through by the pallid limbs. In this welcome shaft, Pibble saw that the two newel posts of the banisters ended in realistically carved animals, an ape and a squirrel.

The light on the second half landing was like a sunburst. Some came from the window, the lower sash of which had been flung up. As the stained glass here depicted "Dante Meeting Beatrice," this meant that the pale, timeless passion-hungry faces were intruded upon by hams and thighs in mauve and emerald tights. But a fiercer, more unnatural light glared from the police photographer's flood lamps, poised above darker patches on the dark red carpet, each patch ringed carefully around with tailor's chalk. An oak cat squatted on one newel, but the other animal was missing.

"We'll come back to this," said Graham. "Scuse me, Jack."

With a patient mumble, the photographer shifted the legs of his tripod to let the two officers pass, and then began to rearrange them. The second landing was a copy of the first, a rectangle with one door at the end and two on either side. All the paintwork was off-chocolate. From somewhere came a tiny, ceaseless muttering, like a mains hum on an old wireless. Graham paused at the second door on the left.

"It's like going into church," he said, "only Dr. Ku says they don't mind. Hope you think we've done right to let them get on with it, Jimmy."

"I'm sure you have."

Graham opened the door.

The caged smells weltered out and mingled in Pibble's nostrils—rugby changing rooms, burnt tires, Italian restaurants, meths, cheap talcum. He went in behind Graham, whose hay-wain figure bulked black for a second against the crazy light. The curtains were drawn. There were seven women in the room, all as dark as anyone Pibble had ever seen. The green flame from a sputtering dish made their skins look midnight blue. They wore jerseys and woolen skirts, but they didn't sit English—they squatted on the floorboards in attitudes which spoke of bare breasts and coarse cotton prints knotted at the waist.

"*Tikaru mindi kmava iraki jissu,*" shrilled the grayhaired one cross-legged at the feet of the corpse.

"*Tikaru mindi kmava iraki hodigu,*" answered a strange lump, featureless with disease, from the far wall.

"*Tikaru mindi kmava iraku mirri,*" cried the next without looking up from the pink sock she was knitting.

"*Tikaru mindi kmava iraku godifadi.*"

"*Tikaru mindi . . .*"

Mindless as the endlessly repeated calls of wild birds, the incantation went on around the circle, and around again. The lump by the far wall rose and threw fresh herbs and a piece of electric cable into the flame. The stench of burnt rubber and strange cooking thickened. Two beldames against the near wall turned a page of the book they held—a Dr. Seuss reading primer—and, finger pointing, started to labor through a fresh sentence; when their turns came, they sang out their responses without looking up. There was no furniture in the room at all. The corpse lay, strictly to attention, in the middle of the floor.

At first, Pibble thought it was a trick of the light that made the victim look so foreshortened, but then he realized the man really was that shape, only just over four feet tall and almost square. His hair was white, in close Negroid curls. The angle from which the light came threw the ritual scarrings on his cheeks into abrupt relief, so that they looked like the lips of small subsidiary mouths, all smiling. The real mouth amid the white beard turned down fiercely at the corners, in the manner of the mask of tragedy on a proscenium arch. The nose was almost flat. The body wore striped pajamas, their colors impossible to be sure of in the grisly light.

Pibble picked his way between the ugly, dusky choristers and knelt by the body. He turned the dead man's head away from him; *rigor* made the left shoulder try to follow the neck with a comedian's baffled shrug. The hair at the back of the skull was stiffened with crusted blood, and a lacy delta marked another flow from the left ear. The skin was barely warmer than the room. Pibble rose and picked his way back; Graham had the door open for him.

They leaned on the landing banisters and peered down into the gloom of the stairwell. To their right, the photographer clicked and fluttered.

"Worth seeing, Jimmy?"

"And smelling. Thank you, Sandy, for the experience. There's a snag about the left-handed blow, I imagine."

"Doesn't mean a thing. Dr. Ku will tell you."

"Know what he was hit with?"

"An owl."

"Off the newel post there?"

"Jimmy, you're a bastard, a gleeking bastard. You might have lifted an eyebrow, for God's sake. How many chances d'you think the average copper gets in his career to tell a colleague that the murderer did the job with an owl?"

"Didn't you tell Pauncefort?" Pibble asked.

"Sergeants don't count."

"Sorry, Sandy. I owe you one double take. No fingerprints or anything, then?"

"Nah. They've seen too much TV. They don't go out much in the evenings, so after seventeen years they know all the tricks. Long before Perry Mason they were watching. Rum do when you think of it—men from Mars, almost—learning all about the great big world outside by staring at the idiot box. Patchy sort of education, but very hot on some things: how to heist a car, or blow a peter, or—"

"Do they side with the Indians against the cowboys?"

"Didn't ask. Anyway, they know all about prints. Finished with that blasted bird, Jack?"

The photographer didn't raise his head from his view finder. "Clean as a whistle," he said, "always excepting the blood. Held with a cloth, my guess."

"Suppose you might as well see it," said Graham to Pibble. "In here."

The owl lay on a marble-topped washstand in the other left-hand room—a small bedroom with an enormous bed. The bird was about fifteen inches high, carved in oak with simple clean strokes which allowed the lines of the grain to suggest the mottling of feathers. There was a little dried blood and a few white hairs behind its right ear, almost as though some enemy had waited for it in the dark and coshed it savagely with a human. Beside it on the marble lay an Edward VII penny.

"That's the *clue*," said Graham disdainfully. He flipped the coin over. On the obverse was the familiar likeness of his late majesty King George V.

Pibble turned it back. There lay the Peacemaker. "Toss you whether it means anything," he said.

"Heads it does. The deceased was holding it so tight that it's left a mark on his palm. I'll show you, if you feel up to facing the Luton Girls' Choir again."

"What did they make of the doctor?"

"Didn't turn a hair. I think they'd have been perfectly happy if he'd got out his little knives and started looking for goodies inside the cadaver, but he didn't. It was Dr. Morton—sound bloke. Says he'd lay heavy odds that there was nothing more to it than a lucky clonk with our feathered friend, or else someone knew exactly where to clonk. About midnight, Morton thinks, on the half landing there. There's a trail of blood, and they found him almost at the top, so he must have crawled on before he died."

Graham pointed to a chalked outline at the edge of the landing where they stood. Pibble walked to the top of the stairs and saw that the marks continued on to the top three steps, making the discernible shape of a human figure, very short and broad. The biggest of the dark patches came where the head would have been.

Graham pointed again, to the half landing below. "There's only one street lamp, so that corner's black as pitch, Dr. Ku says, even with the window open. It was last night. Our chap could have stood in the corner waiting for the old boy to come up the stairs. He always went pretty slowly, hauling on the banisters—bad heart. Easy to clock him as he passed."

"They've learned about footmarks from the telly, too?" Pibble asked.

"Course. The whole corner's wiped clean. He used the lace doo-day from the window, and then just left it lying on the sill. Wiped the sill, too, for some reason."

"Came from outside, perhaps."

"Leaned on the sill for a bit, more like, watching for the old boy to come home."

"He went out in those pajamas?" Pibble asked.

"That's right. Never wore anything else, the Kus say. Just put more layers of pajamas on when the weather turned colder. You've got to realize, Jimmy, that until he was forty-odd he didn't wear anything most days."

"Yes, of course. Did he go out much?"

"That's about as far as I got when I decided to ask for you. Dr. Ku will tell you the rest. I'll introduce you and be off. We've got a nasty bit of kid-molesting up by St. Stephen's— run-o'-the-mill, really, but it's got me bothered."

"I know what you mean, Sandy. It's quaint, like an exercise in a forgotten art form. You go and harry your pervert with a clear conscience. Where's Dr. Ku?"

"Floor below."

They had to wait. The photographer had achieved a delicate and contorted balance of himself and his tripod, both cantilevered across the stairwell, to photograph the owl's abandoned pedestal from a rewarding angle. Pibble might have edged past, but for Graham to have tried would have risked both man and machine. Sandy looks edgy, thought Pibble. Hope he's all right. Enough prima donnas in the force already. Odd how little you can hear from the wake room—or smell, either. He left the banisters to look at the door. It wasn't what he'd expected, a flimsy old deal affair with fillets of fresh wood tacked to the top to fill successive gaps caused by a subsiding doorpost; no, it was solid mahogany, four-square, fitting its frame as closely as the air lock on a spaceship. Pibble leaped a few inches into the air and came down on his heels; the floor scarcely gave, though the photographer glanced around, frowning, and then (seeing that the tremor had been caused by a senior officer) erased all emotion from his face.

"Sorry," said Pibble.

"That's all right, sir. I'd finished. It was just the principle of the thing."

"Sturdy bit of building this, Sandy. Last for a thousand years if they don't pull it down. Funny the way they used to put top-class craftsmanship into such hideous buildings sometimes. Stairs don't creak, doors almost soundproof. Ideal setup for an ambush."

"Yes. Come on." From Graham's tone, Pibble half expected him to add, "Let's get it over."

On the floor below, Graham knocked at the single door at the far end of the landing, waited respectfully for an answer, and went in. In its way, the room was almost as improbable, in that particular house, as the wake room on the floor above. It was large, and brimming with light. Two tall windows opened onto back gardens where Pibble could see the top of a savagely over-pollarded sycamore. Both the big neon lights in the ceiling were on, and auxiliary illumination came from a Swedish-looking standard lamp, which must have had at least two 150-watt bulbs in it, and a couple of angle-poises. There couldn't have been a shadow anywhere. The furniture was too low, curveless modern sofas, a large architect's desk, and several silly gilt chairs, upright, such as one used to see in the tearooms of would-be smart cinemas. The fabrics were soft grays and yellows, which made the pictures all the more staring.

Eight canvases hung on the walls, and a pile of others was stacked in a corner. They were all the same size, tall and narrow, and all unframed; Pibble liked them quite a lot. The colors were fierce and simple, giving, at first glance, an impression that the pictures were gaudy abstracts. Then, in a blink, he saw that this was caused by the carefully formal patterning of the backgrounds, and that each picture was a portrait of a person or an animal—naïve but not childlike. There was no hesitation anywhere. The insides of the creatures were drawn as if they were on the outside. There was a heron with a fish in its stomach. There was a European businessman with bowler, brolly, and blue pin-stripe; you could see both his wallet and his esophagus. Pibble nearly laughed aloud with pleasure.

Behind the desk, a very black black man sat stabbing at the wood with a scribing knife. A red-haired white woman sat on the sofa in front of Sandy. She had a square, soft face and was dressed wholly in black—high-necked jersey, ski trousers, ballet shoes. She looked fortyish, and sat peculiarly still and upright.

Sandy's attitude was peculiar, too; while Pibble looked at the pictures, he embarked on a series of gaunt banalities, his accent becoming more Scottish with every sentence. The woman assented at intervals with a slow nod of her head.

Sandy said, for instance, that it was fine the noo, but likely there'd be thunder betimes. He looked smaller but more ungainly, and if he'd had a cap he'd have been twiddling it in front of his crotch. Ah well, thought Pibble, every man to his own terrors—*that's* why he sent for me so promptly. Is it just her slinky, sub-masculine style that does it, or has she got something else on him? Anyway, who am I to deride?

Sandy plodded around to the point at last.

"This is Detective Superintendent Pibble from the Yard, Ma'am," he said. "He will be able to devote his whole time to resolving your difficulties, which I canna. I've known him a long time."

Like an undergardener giving a good character for one of his mates at the Big House. The woman replied in the same idiom.

"Thank you very much, Mr. Graham. You have already given us more of your time than we deserve, and you have been very tolerant of our eccentricities. We must not detain you any longer from clearing up that unpleasant business at St. Stephen's, which you must consider more important than our irrelevant little tragedy here."

Pibble tried to place the accent—not that you could call it an accent by the broad standards of B.B.C. regional programs—rather an intonation, a slight clipping, a narrowing of the vowels, a hint that in her cups the lady might begin to lilt. Edinburgh! The great dames of that city—the wives of Writers to the Signet, the sisters of successive Provosts—exchange the gossip of their exclusive society in just such tones over tiny cups of lemon tea—or used to, forty years ago. Surely, thought Pibble, they can't have survived the intervening slumps and wars and Socialist governments untouched. Still, no wonder Sandy was twiddling his invisible cap, as though it were *he* who had slain the old man, by knocking his ball through the irreplaceable windows, and was now come to own up and offer to pay for the damage, week by week, out of his pocket money. Sandy came from a decent Edinburgh family, but not that rarefied. Pibble decided to try and jolt the conversation into the sixties.

"Superintendent Graham says you can give me the dope on the setup here. The sooner I get stuck into it, the more chance I've got of making some sense of it."

"Quite right, Mr. Pibble," said the woman. "Goodbye, Mr. Graham. I am sure your colleague will keep you *au fait* with whatever progress he may make."

"Sure," said Pibble.

"Goodbye, Ma'am," said Graham. "Goodbye, Mr. Ku. James, you will be in touch with me?"

"Sure," said Pibble, who was called James about once in two years, mostly by some senile cousin. Graham left.

"Now see what you've done," said the black man. His voice was very deep and rich. "You've alienated the new Superintendent by teasing the old one. What you have to explain is already sufficiently complex without your introducing adventitious complexities."

"I'm sorry," said Dr. Ku. "I was so scared when I started speaking to him that I suppose I instinctively imitated Mummy, and he reacted so strongly that it would have made things worse if I'd stopped. Can we start all over again, Superintendent Pibble? It will relieve you of the obligation to lard your interrogation with slang."

"I'm easy either way," said Pibble. "Why were you frightened of Superintendent Graham?"

There were several odd intangible things about her. The first one Pibble pinned down was that she sat stiller than anyone he'd ever seen before.

"Oh," she said, "I was not frightened of him—merely frightened. It is not simply that the idea of anyone of our community killing Aaron is horrifying. As an anthropologist,

I would have thought it impossible. But it seems equally impossible that anyone should have come from outside and done it. And he was struck with the left hand, and with a piece of wood lying by the path."

"What does that mean?" said Pibble. "Graham told me there was something funny about the left-hand business."

"Yes. To start with, Superintendent, you must realize that we are all members of the same tribe. We come from New Guinea. Ku is not really a surname, but what we call ourselves in our own language. We are the sole survivors of our own civilization, the only living Kus—the rest were obliterated by the Japanese. We are, even by the standards of Central New Guinea, a very primitive people, and the whole of our behavior patterns is riddled with ritual and tabu. There is almost no predicament—certainly no predicament with which we might be faced in our own jungle—for which we have not a prescribed mode of action. The predicament of killing a member of our own tribe is one. This we would invariably do with the left hand, and with a chance piece of wood or a stone picked up by our path. It would be the deepest pollution of our real weapons, and hence of our manhood, to use one of them to kill a Ku."

"The same applies to the women?"

"They would not own weapons, of course. But they would use the left hand."

Mr. Ku stopped stabbing the desk. "Are you certain of that, Eve?" His bass was theatrical, a voice like drums.

Dr. Ku answered in a foreign language, one full of dentals and labials, with complex vowels strung together into immense polysyllables, singsongy. Mr. Ku boomed back in kind, but in his voice the consonants merely fluttered above a velvet thorough bass of sound. Dr. Ku shook her head and settled the argument in a couple of sentences that were like a flight of improbable birds.

"We must apologize," said Mr. Ku. "The affairs of our people make better sense in our own speech. Eve was reminding me of an episode in the life of my maternal grandfather. The women would kill a Ku with the left hand also. It is true."

"You both seem," said Pibble, "to take the idea of killing a Ku calmly enough, yet you think it impossible that a Ku should have done this particular murder."

"Both attitudes are valid," said Mr. Ku.

"To us," said Dr. Ku. "But it is not to be expected that they should be to you, Mr. Pibble. In general, throughout New Guinea internecine killing is not a rarity. The killing of a chief (and Aaron was our chief) by a member of his own clan is much rarer, and there is no tradition of its having happened among the Kus. Furthermore, there is a statistical relationship, on which I have published a paper myself, between internecine killing and the well-being of a clan. In short, there are two phases in which the vast majority of such killings occur—first, when the clan population is appreciably above its norm and approaches the limits which the tribal area can support in comfort, but when, for one of a number of reasons, it has not proved possible to resort to the usual expedient of warfare; second, when the clan population diminishes to a point where the clan itself begins to lose its sense of identity and becomes, you might say, psychopathic. We, of course, are very much closer to the second state than the first, but now that the children are beginning to grow up we are nothing like as close as we were. Not, I assure you, that that means we have been through a period when murders were the regular thing; but we have endured a climate in which it was theoretically possible for murder to occur, and now I believe the climate to be different. As an anthropologist, I would be astonished if Aaron had been killed by a Ku. But, as a practical person living in this house and knowing Aaron,

I cannot believe that he was killed by some intruder. Paul will confirm what I have said."

The black man smiled. In that squashed and alien face, it was impossible to tell what the smile meant—sympathy, shyness, hypocrisy, the instinctive rictus of a carnivore moving on its prey, anything.

"Yes," he said. "Eve knows us. In my marrow, I am certain that I could not have killed Aaron, and nor could any of us."

Hmm, thought Pibble, this is right nasty. What have we here but a very sophisticated version of "Oh, Orficer, it can't 'ave bin one of the fambly as done it, reely it can't. It must 'ave been some 'orrible man what broke in." What can one do but raise an eyebrow? He raised it.

"Perhaps," said Dr. Ku, "you had better cable Professor Fleisch at Melbourne. He will confirm the theoretical background. Paul's marrow you will have to take on trust."

"I'm afraid I can't take anything on trust. Let's start at another point. The deceased was out in his pajamas. He can't have gone far. Have you any idea where he went?"

"The odds are he was visiting the Caines. He liked to chat with Susan, especially when Bob wasn't there."

"The Caines?"

"Bob and Susan Caine live next door. We know them well, though we have not known Susan very long. They were married only last year, but Susan was a tremendous help when we had an outbreak of scarlet fever in the winter. We have known Bob much longer. He was with us in the valley. It was because of him . . ."

She sat as still as ever, but the precise voice stumbled. Two lines of strain seamed the pale flesh beside her mouth. Mr. Ku's deep accents moved gently into the silence.

"Eve means that our tribe was destroyed because Bob

Caine was there. He was the catalyst. It was not his fault, but we are tied to him with a strong rope."

Pibble went to the door and called. Graham had left in such a dither that they hadn't discussed what forces Pibble could dispose of, but there must be someone. Feet thudded up from the jungly gloom of the hall. A minion, by Jove!

"Did Superintendent Graham leave anyone else behind?"

"Yessir. Strong, sir. And he said to apologize we weren't more. My name's Fernham, sir."

"Did either of you do the early round of the Terrace, scouting for witnesses, Constable?"

"Both of us, sir. That's why the Superintendent left us. It's mostly flats, and o' course we didn't get an answer from about half of them, and nothing useful from those as *did* answer."

"Were the Caines, next door, in?"

"Which side, sir?"

"Number eight, basement," called Dr. Ku from inside the room. "I think Bob's away at the moment, and Susan usually does her shopping early. If she was out, she should be back by now."

"Right, Constable," said Pibble. "Nip down there again, will you, and if Mrs. Caine's in ask her whether the deceased visited her last night. Find out about times, subject of visit, suchlike."

"Yessir."

"If he did visit the Caines," said Pibble as he came back into the room, "would he have left the door unlocked?"

"Certainly not. He had a key."

"So for the murder to have been done by an outsider he would either have had to break in, and Superintendent Graham would have told me if there'd been any sign of that; or he'd have had to come in earlier in the day and lurked about;

or he'd have had to have a key of his own. Do any of these possibilities seem likely to you?"

"None," said Dr. Ku. "The lurking intruder is most implausible. Europeans have a very distinctive smell, for one thing. Nor is the door, as you imply, left on the latch all day. This is not a hotel; it is a private house."

Pibble was pleased by the rebuke. He liked Dr. Ku considerably. Her primness of speech was part of her offbeat attractiveness, and she looked very cool, in control, but seriously concerned—a thoroughly proper attitude for somebody in whose house a nasty little murder has been committed.

Or was the propriety, the donnishness, the almost phony primness, just a barricade against the nastiness—and not a very effective one at that? She had crumpled completely, a moment back, at the first mention of the Caine figure.

"O.K.," he said. "I don't go much on the lurking intruder either. We'll bear him in mind but look for something more likely. Who has a key to the house, for instance, and how many have been lost in the past six months or so?"

"All the adults have keys," said Dr. Ku. "None has ever been lost. The basement door is always bolted and the front door has a good Ingersoll lock."

"None lost! But there must be a dozen of you!"

"Seventeen. I fear I must do my professional act again. Among a people like the Kus, Superintendent, ritual has a meaning as solid as the meaning of a rates demand to you. You must know people who carry a lucky charm about, or swear by some mascot—they'd be distressed if they lost it, but still in their hearts they would know that their penchant for their own little totem was just a whimsical superstition, perhaps with psychological overtones. This would not be a conceivable attitude of mind for us. There are many objects to which we attach a ritual—you would say 'magical'—significance which to us is solid and real. For instance, some shapes of cooking pot are used only in the preparation of great feasts, not for good luck or custom's sake, but because the pot is part of the feast, quite as much as the meat that is stewed in it.

"The keys have this nature, too. I expect you can imagine what a psychological turmoil our removal to England involved—the shouting and jostling; the meaningless, unpatterned behavior of people; the new and repugnant smells; the very horizons changing from day to day, as though the hard hills were wavering like smoke. And then to come here, to be given a little magical gadget with which it was possible to shut out utterly all that imbecile flux, so that we could begin to build up again the known and detailed pattern of daily behavior. If you said the keys symbolized our membership of the Ku clan (what is left of it), you would be wrong— they *are* our membership. It has not happened yet, so I cannot be certain, but I seriously think that if one of us was to lose his key outside the house he would refuse to come home. He would, in a sense, have lost his identity. Do you agree, Paul?"

Mr. Ku replied in his own tongue, his velvet bass sounding less truly exotic in those thickets of sound than it did in English.

"Paul thinks," said Dr. Ku, "that if one of us lost his key outside he *would* come home, but would then (voluntarily, though it would be expected of him) undergo a reinitiation ritual which is both protracted and uncomfortable. Paul may be right—I tend to take a melodramatic view of our affairs at times. But either way you will understand why no keys have been lost."

"Yes," said Pibble. "But you must see that that disposes of the third method by which an outsider might have got in, unless he was a skilled professional thief—and skilled thieves have their own tabus. You'll have to take my word for it, but they would be most unlikely to kill an old man going upstairs. Another thing: you said that the Kus would most likely smell a stranger in the house. Wouldn't Aaron have smelled whoever was waiting to ambush him, if it had not been one of you?"

"I had thought of that," said Mr. Ku. "He had got over his cold, I think."

Dr. Ku said nothing. Her silence was not sulky or obstinate, but the contained blankness of someone who has nothing, for the moment, to add. She sat totally still, like a priest in contemplation, a mathematician staring at the grained surface of his desk, an ape in the sun.

"So you see," intruded Pibble, "my first step must be to sort out and eliminate, as far as possible, the actual inmates of the house. As there are so many, it would be best if we could have a sort of informal parade—in here, for preference—so that I can see who's who and ask a few straightforward questions, if you will interpret for me. D'you think you could get them down here?"

Dr. Ku sighed.

"I think," she said, "they all speak sufficient English for your needs, but you misunderstand my position here. I'm afraid I am a very inferior sort of creature in the hierarchy—Paul, too. I had a lot of influence with Aaron, because of my father, but now I do not know. I certainly cannot order the rest of the tribe to come and go."

"Because you are a woman?"

"No—it is more complicated than that, and peculiarly interesting to an anthropologist. Technically I am a man. When my father and Moses decided that some of the Kus should go into hiding, my mother insisted that I should go with them. My father was against it, but agreed on condition that I was accepted into the tribe as a man. I was about seventeen, but it wasn't only in case I got raped at the next feast; as a man, I would have some say in the councils of the group in hiding, and Aaron would be able to consult with me, which he could not decently have done with a woman. It was a sensible arrangement, though it has led to awkwardnesses."

"But how does that affect—"

"It is my relationship with Paul that has diminished my authority, Superintendent. This, naturally, the Kus regard as a homosexual relationship. The attitude of different societies to homosexuality is extremely varied; some regard it as normal, others as despicable. There are still a few places where it is punished by death. Among the Kus and related tribes, random homosexuality is rare and severely punished, but for two men to become steadfast lovers is regarded as only mildly despicable—indeed a trifle comic. Paul and I come in for a lot of banter on feast days, but it is good-natured enough. Still, we have forfeited our full membership of the men's hut; we cannot join in discussions and parliaments. At the time, it seemed to resolve a number of difficulties, both personal and tribal, so Paul and I decided on what is, in the tribe's eyes, a homosexual marriage. Of course there are prescribed rituals for this, which we carefully observed."

11

Eve squatted under the fig tree, worrying. It was dusk for a few minutes before the huge-starred night; the hummingbirds were gone, and a fruit bat was out and flopping among the upper leaves. Eve was sentry. Nobody had seen a Japanese for a fortnight, but she was glad to be alone. The facile joke of being a man was wearing thin, with the hiding lasting so long. There were too few women in the caves, and the others knew she wasn't *really* a man, despite her hurried initiation, because she bore no ritual scars. She was a sort of nobody, of no sex. When the hunters' awe for her father had melted a bit further—a few days would do it—she would be in a real jam.

Odds were the full-moon feast would be the night when she stopped being a person and became some hunter's animated chattel. The feast would be a hole-and-corner do, compared with the old junketings in the village, but even Aaron would be roaring drunk. Five days. If nothing changed, she'd run away on the fourth. If Bob weren't so sick, he'd help—or would he? He might think it a great big joke. What about trying to rig some ghostlike manifestation of Daddy, to renew the old respect? Possible, but it would mean props—the hat, the jacket. It would mean going to the village. Before she could draw down the blinds in her skull, she pictured the garroted bodies dangling in the charred doorways. No props, then, and no ghosts.

She was damned if she was going to try and make herself

look more like a man. The bandage around her breasts hurt all day, and anyway it wouldn't be any use. She was already so hideous by Ku standards, so unlike the huge-haunched, long-breasted, slab-shaped women of their dreams, that even if she was to grow a mustache and sing bass she couldn't make herself less sexually attractive. But all a drunk Ku needed on a feast night was the minimum equipment.

Surely Aaron was worried, too. He might think up some tabu valid enough to be potent after gourdfuls of vile, sweet *kava*. No rigging of the spirit world for him, though: it was all too real for cheating. But he might pull something out of the bag still. Or what about Bob again? Was his sickness real? There weren't any symptoms you could see, but it might be shock. Anyway, chattel or no chattel, could she really run off and leave him after all that had happened? Or what about Paul. . . .

A hand touched her arm, in the crook of the bare flesh inside the elbow. Jiminy, how quietly they could all move! She looked sideways and up, through the dark. It was Paul, naked, carrying his short bow. He leaned it against the tree and squatted beside her. Silence.

From behind his ear Paul drew what looked like a fat twig and handed it to Eve. It was softer than branch wood—a root. Eve turned it in her hands.

"What does this mean, Paul?"

"Miss, Aaron say—if we are man and man—loving—we may not go to moon feast."

Silence. Good Paul. Quiet, attentive, reserved, the perfect houseboy. Only there was now no house. The star pupil. And no school either. It was a way out. There had been a homosexual couple in the village, middle-aged, very good hunters. They had been set apart. Yes. Paul's English had been better down in the village—was he rusty, or just embarrassed? No telling. Presumably he'd not spoken Ku because he wanted to make sure she understood what he was suggesting.

"Like David and Jonathan, Paul?"

"Yes, Miss."

"What do we do?"

"We break root. We bite. I bite, you bite. We put our bitings into other one's mouth. They make our mouth blue, so all Kus can know we are man and man, loving."

Oh, the white wedding in St. Andrew's, with the bridesmaids all in satin and the black coats and the flowered hats and the organ playing "Love Divine."

The root was like alum, drying the mouth. It took a lot of chewing.

"Is finished, Miss."

"Call me Eve, Paul. Now we're man and man, loving. Let's go and set up house."

III

Pibble looked at the poised head; the soft, secretive brown eyes; the Edinburgh-straight back; the unmitigated black attire. Very embraceable, the whole effect—a challenge to male domination; his sort of woman, except that she wouldn't have him. Doesn't look as if she *needed* anything, he thought. Rum do, all around. Wonder who does what and with what and to whom. Probably tell you, if you asked—no, probably not. It'd be beyond the line of scholarly interest. Still, no wonder she takes a wog-bashing so calmly. Would *anything* dismay her? No goblin or foul fiend, anyway.

"I see. Can you tell me, Dr. Ku, whether the owl had any ritual significance?"

She turned slowly toward her black man. Their eyes met. He shrugged his shoulders and she turned back, slow as a priest at Mass, to Pibble.

"If it has," she said, "neither Paul nor I know of it, though we are not especially adept in the women's lore. It was the only loose animal on the stairs, too."

"Um. And the two-headed penny the deceased was clutching?"

"A two-headed penny!"

"Yes. He was—"

Knock on the door. Enter Fernham, excited.

"Sorry to butt in, sir, but deceased spent an hour with Mrs. Caine last night. She just got back, sir, and she didn't know what had happened. She's a bit upset, sir."

"Say anything useful?"

"She thinks he left about eleven-twenty, sir. She says he often used to come and talk—mostly about his home. I didn't like to badger her, sir; she was crying and I thought I'd better give her a chance to pull herself together. Then I thought you'd like to see her yourself, sir."

"Right. Thank you, Constable. If she's back, some of the others may be. Would you and Strong do the rounds again and check the people who were missing first go? In fact, you'd better do the whole lot, now you know about the time. Make a note of any kids of courting age—they hang about in porches all hours—not that they'd be any use as witnesses about time. Or anything else, really."

"Righty-ho, sir."

Fernham was gone, leaving in the air the inaudible echoes of a phrase that always set Pibble's teeth on edge. He turned to Dr. Ku, and was surprised not to find in her eyes the hint of a similar distaste. Perhaps she hadn't heard, in her trance of stillness.

"Dr. Ku," he said, "I can't really believe that your influence on the household is as small as you make out, and in any case you could always say you were simply passing my orders on. It would be true. So would you arrange for everybody to be in one room—one with a bit of light in it, like this—in half an hour? If you've time, I'd be most grateful for a list of their names, with any relevant notes."

"I could get out the cards from my index."

"That'd do fine. And—it probably hasn't got anything to do with the killing, but you can't be sure—a résumé of the financial setup here."

Again came the slow turn toward Paul, the shrug, the slow turn back.

"I don't see why not, Superintendent."

"Fine. I'll be back in half an hour, if you can get everyone on parade by then. Or will the ceremony upstairs not be finished?"

"Oh," said Dr. Ku, "that will end as soon as the body is taken away. I had imagined that the police would have done that by now."

"Um. I have a feeling that Superintendent Graham will have told his chaps not to barge in until the ladies had finished whatever they're up to."

Mr. Ku laughed sourly and suddenly. "Superintendent, it would be a kindness to intrude. We are like children, easily bored, even by prolonged excitement."

"I'll see what I can do."

The landing and stairs seemed black after that glaring room; the daylight striking through the anatomy of "Love Locked Out" gave, for the moment, no more illumination than the moon throws on the floor of a thick-leaved wood. Pibble stared at the picture while his eyes became used to the dusk. A fixed window, he noticed, not a sash—no chance here of a desire for daylight throwing those pale limbs into obscene confusion. There was a figure on the lower stairs now— a still white face, black body, black additional head under the right arm. Ah, yes, a uniformed man carrying his helmet.

"Strong, isn't it?"

"It is, sir."

"I'm going next door, to the basement of Number eight, for about half an hour. There are three things I'd like you to do. First, get hold of the mortuary van and tell them they can take the body away. They needn't mind the goings on in the room, provided they act a bit reverent. Second, sort out where I'm going to have lunch—a Whitbread pub for preference, though a Courage or a Charrington would do. I don't want to have to go hunting round. Make up my mind for me. Third, get hold of Fernham—he's out in the Terrace somewhere—and arrange to search the whole building five minutes after I come back. I'll be holding a parade of the inmates in Dr. Ku's room, and I want to be sure no one's missing. Got that?"

"Got it, sir. Remove cadaver, recommend pub, search premises." The blond beard wagged, as if ticking the points off. "You going to see Mrs. Caine, sir?"

"You know her?"

"I do, sir. Nice bit of crackling, she is—underneath it all. Came up to the station February asking after a lost set of keys, and dropped in a question or two, all casual, about her husband. Been missing a few days, apparently, but she wasn't worrying. She said."

"Thank you, Strong. Don't forget about the pub. Good bitter, fresh bread, mousetrap, bangers."

May, out in the street, seemed as solid as stone compared to the imported and crazily preserved tropics inside No. 9. The murder, in that hard sunlight, became hallucinatory and trivial, except that for the moment it was Pibble's job. Next week, like as not, he'd be off at the other end of London puzzling out what sort of twist in the mind could make a chap take to strangling whores with college scarves. Two pigeons strutted through their clockwork courtship on the crown of the asphalt, their shot-silk necks arched with appreciation of each other's efforts, he to pursue, she to stay six inches out of reach. Silently Pibble cheered his own sex on. A pram had appeared on the far pavement. Things hadn't changed so much—it was a streamlined, two-toned job in white and lavender, chromed unsparingly, the bodywork bulging just below the handles into a pair of simulated jet exhausts. Its occupant, by a happy fluke, was crying at a pitch that was just right for a tiny aero engine screaming for take-off.

Conscientiously Pibble stubbed out his moment of Words-worthian insight. He turned right and down the steps to the basement of No. 8. No milk empties down here, or wet rubbish in corners. The wall that retained the road was pale pink; a wooden name plate, "8a Cora Lynn," hung on two tiny chains from the peak of the ogee arch that supported the steps up to the porch of No. 8 proper; the door of the basement flat was lime green and open.

Pibble went in and found a hall decorated with a brilliant Paisley wallpaper, the one Sanderson's had just begun to use in their glossiest ads. A turquoise door on the left of the passage opened, and a girl said, "Come in."

It was the kitchen. Red lino, yellow walls and cupboards, two big orange Goods and Chattels posters filling gaps. All the equipment cheap and old, but very clean and tidy.

The girl—woman—no, girl—was a surprise for being a girl at all. Somehow Pibble expected everybody involved in the case to be at least in their late thirties. That obliterated village in the jungle valley already loomed so large that he felt it off-key that even such a chance and peripheral witness as Mrs. Caine should clearly not have been born when the thatch went up in flames. Her eyes had the large, soft look that very strong spectacles give—ultrasevere National Health specs in this case. Her head was tiny and very round, with a tiny, pretty nose and mouth below the enormous eyes; the hair an off-mouse bob; the body plump and cuddly in its knitted beige dress.

"You're the Superintendent," she said. Her voice had the sharp reasonableness of a career businesswoman in a B film. "I know I'll have to tell at least six different people the same things before I'm done, so I shan't mind if you ask exactly the same questions as the other bod. Couldn't they do this part of detecting by computer, and save all the overlapping which we ratepayers cough up for?"

"I suppose it might work," said Pibble, "if you could program it for the rumness of people. Difficult to prepare in advance for a setup like next door, don't you think? And that lot's only unique in a rather exotic way on the surface—half the households in London turn out to be just as off-center once you do a bit of digging. Do you know them well?"

"Eve and her Kus? As well as anybody, I suppose, except Bob, though I've only known them for ten months. But it depends what you mean by *know*. I saw a lot of poor old Aaron, for instance, but I couldn't've told whether he was happy or unhappy at any given moment. Do you think one of the Kus killed him?"

"What do *you* think? Dr. Ku seems to regard it as anthropologically impossible."

"I simply can't keep up with Eve on that sort of thing, but I thought they were mostly pretty fond of the old boy, and respectful as all getout. It was funny. My dad's a fairly high-powered figure in the Navy, and the way the other Kus treated Aaron reminded me of the way the middies used to behave with Dad when he was a captain. But I've no idea what they felt individually—I still can't tell one or two of them apart, and nor can Bob, though he's known them twenty years."

"Well, what about Dr. Ku? D'you think she'd tell me if she knew who'd done it? Or if she knew of a motive?"

"She's not much more scrutable, is she, Superintendent? I don't think she would. I don't want to be bitchy, and anyway Eve's a sort of saint in some ways, but she's funny about the Kus. Bob says she thinks they're her own private stamp collection, unique, worth untold millions in auction rooms, not to be touched by ignorant hands. Besides, I'm sure she thinks their laws are as valid as ours. You'll have to ask Bob. He ought to be back soon."

"Where's he been?"

"Off on a business trip somewhere. He doesn't always tell me where he's going. He's got some agencies for Swedish

firms in the south of England, and has to go and persuade
factory owners in Swindon that they'd be better off with his
sort of industrial filter, or whatever it is. It makes for an
unsettled life, rather, but it suits him."

"Anyway, he wasn't in London last night?"

"Good Lord, no, or he'd have been here. And Aaron
wouldn't have come round. They didn't get on, though Bob
will never tell me why. It wasn't anything *serious*, Superintendent, not a *mote*. . . ." The sharp voice became fainter
and more urgent. "You'd better ask him; he'd tell *you*. Look,
Superintendent, I *must* start getting him some luncheon ready,
just in case he turns up. He never has any breakfast, you see,
so he gets pretty famished by now. But carry on—I can
answer questions while I cope."

Cope was the word. Pibble sat on a tall stool by the sink
and watched Mrs. Caine tip her string bag of groceries onto
the yellow Formica of the table in a sharp, practiced movement, like a coal heaver tipping his sackful down a manhole:
a few tins, a green pepper, a hundred Senior Service, butter,
soup packets, streaky bacon, macaroni. Without moving her
feet, she took a knife from a drawer and a chopping board
off the shelf behind her. She sliced the pepper into coarse
strips, slowly, as though it were vital that every strip should
be the same precise width.

"I don't know that I've got a lot else to ask you, Mrs.
Caine. I hear that Aaron didn't talk about anything that he
mightn't have talked about on any other evening, and that
he left at about eleven-twenty."

"That's right."

"What did he talk about, in fact?"

"New Guinea. He always did. What it was like, and
whether they would ever go back there. They'd seen some
sort of exploring film on the telly a few weeks back, and they
were desperately stirred up—the old ones, anyway. There'd

been a village just like theirs. I don't think there was a serious possibility of their going, but it gave them something to talk about."

The strips of pepper went into melted butter in a frying pan; a saucepan was filled with water, presumably for macaroni. Mrs. Caine managed to cook as if she knew precisely what she was at, and with very few movements. Now she started to open a tin of stewed steak with an old-fashioned, pre-butterfly can opener, the sort you have to wrestle with. She wrestled clumsily, and Pibble was just about to do the honorable thing and take the job on himself when she jabbed her left thumb with the spike of the instrument.

"I'm an idiot," she said, and ran cold water on it. "There's some Elastoplast in the top left cupboard behind you, on the second shelf."

There was, too. None of Mary's in-the-thing-behind-the-thing-over-there-I-think. Dear God, an unself-conscious jewel. He stripped the plastic protection from the sticky surface and smoothed the plaster around the strong, small thumb. It curved very sharply back and its nail was bitten flat down to the skin.

A voice came from the door.

"Ullo, ullo! The other fellah caught in the nest, eh?"

Pibble turned and saw his destined Adversary. He knew him at once, and his innards cringed, the creature of his waking nightmares, poised to demolish whatever he began or undertook—always the same, with the same lounging arrogance, the same Olympian sneer. The nightmare became real only once in a couple of years, and this, now, here, was one of the times.

The Adversary's smile was genial, denying the hint of cruelty in the words. Even teeth flashed; brown eyes crinkled at the corners. The clothes were sharp and modern, a chocolate-brown suit with its waistcoat buttoned high, and on the notch of pink shirt a patently club tie. Everything about him suited him, even the bruise-colored sacs below his eyes and the alcohol hoarseness of his voice.

"Darling," said Mrs. Caine, "I've got the most awful news. Somebody murdered Aaron Ku last night, hit him on the head on the stairs, and this is the Detective Superintendent who is trying to find out what happened."

"Christ! Who'd want to bash old Aaron? Poor old black bastard."

"Darling, why don't you take the Superintendent into your study and tell him all he wants to know about the Kus. You understand them much better than anyone. And I'll get on with luncheon."

"Right. Come along, copper."

"Is your thumb all right, Mrs. Caine? Shall I finish off the tin for you?"

"Good God! Cut yourself, Sue? PERFECT WOMAN SLIPS SENSATION! I must make a note in my diary."

"Off you go, Bob, or you won't get any lunch."

"Aye aye, Cap'n. Come along, copper. You married, old man?"

They moved out into the passage, Pibble sweating lightly. Caine's aggressive, self-assured charm reminded him of Walewski, the big docker with a knack of knocking his women about in a way that hardly marked them at all, though they might have to go to hospital for months. Walewski had enjoyed his art, certain that none of the women would ever give evidence against him. He'd been right—their terrified fascination with him, all five or six of the ones Pibble had met, had been wholly police-proof. It had been a couple of kids, that blond Mavis Something's little brothers, who'd sent Walewski down—them and the prosecution lawyer who'd talked to one of the doctors and become sufficiently angry. Pibble had given evidence, and Walewski had smiled from the dock all the time, a smile that said clear as shouting, "You haven't a hope, you poor little runt." Eighteen months Walewski had got, trapped in the net of the law, too stupid to see that this was something different from the jungle in which he lived his strong, cruel tiger life.

Caine's study was on the other side of the passage, a tiny room, intensely and intentionally masculine. The only decoration was an enormously blown-up photograph of Caine, taped to a wall; it showed him spread-eagled on a face of rock, apparently leading a climb, as a slack of rope dangled downward from his waist and no rope led up. His face was turned sideways so that the craggy profile showed to full advantage. He was laughing like a businessman at a floor show. 'Twas very theatric.

A pair of climbing boots hung from a nail on another wall and a coil of nylon rope lay in a corner. Caine picked up a shiny *piton* from the desk and plonked it in the middle of a loose pile of papers.

"Funny how cleaning women can't put things back," he said, "however much they love you."

Without apology, he laid himself full length in the only chair, a vanquished object with a torn cover. The seat's edge supported the small of his back, his crossed legs stuck out four feet across the room, his head was on a level with the arms of the chair, and his neck was bent almost to a right angle by the back of it. He looked as though he and a few friends owned the world. Pibble decided that he would feel less abject perching on the edge of the desk than standing subservient before this arrogant layabout.

"Sorry, copper, I didn't catch your name."

"I am Detective Superintendent Pibble, C.I.D." The only refuge was police-college formality. "As a preliminary, may I ask where you yourself spent last night?"

"You may, cock. I was in Southampton, at Turner's Hotel

in Crerdon Road, the meanest bleeding doss house this side
of Timbuktu."

"Did you go down by car?"

"Can't afford to run one, old boy—not anything I'd be prepared to be seen dead in. I've got a cobber in the trade who
lends me a decent piece of iron from time to time, but I
don't care to ask too often. I took out a beaut of a two-point-
three Alfa last weekend, got her up to twenty over the ton
on the M4—not bad for 1930, eh?"

"How long have you known the Kus?"

"Twenty-five years ago this June, I staggered into their
village, copper, pretty sick, and with a duff ankle, too. Been
in that bleeding jungle four days, scuttling under cover when
a leaf rattled. They were good to me, those Kus, though I
sometimes think they'd rather have eaten me than nursed me
—probably would have if the Rev. hadn't been there in his
crazy old hat. Eve's dad, that was, and as near a saint as
I'm ever likely to meet on this bleeding piece of earth. Then
they all had to go and get themselves wiped out by the
stinking Nips. If there was a God in heaven . . ."

His voice ran into the sand. For the last few sentences, he
had been talking like a maudlin drunk, whose pity for the
world is only his pity for himself. He looked as if he'd had a
thickish night—perhaps there was enough alcohol still in his
system for shock to bring it to the surface.

"Have you been with them ever since?" asked Pibble.

"Pretty near. I went back to Australia for a year or two
after the show was over, but I kept worrying about little
Eve being all alone in the world, so I did a bit of sleuthing,
found she'd come back here, and set up camp next door. She
may look a pretty tough egg, but she needs a man handy.
She's not practical. D'you know how she spent the first eight
years after she got back? Slaving at her schoolbooks, matric-
ulating, getting her degree, getting her goddam doctorate.

Eve set a great store by that—owed it to her dad, I think she thinks. By the same token, she takes all her tribe off in a crazy crocodile to church every Sunday."

"They are Christians, then?" Did the façade of formality hide his astonishment? With luck it did, Pibble decided; Caine was too self-absorbed to take much note of enemy reactions. Pibble recalled the whining, boring chant in the blue-green light of the wake room. *Jissu. Hodigu. Mirri. Godifadi!* The blessed Trinity and the Mother of God, all translated.

"I understand from Dr. Ku that she does not exercise any real authority over the Kus," he said.

"Not bleeding likely! It's her house, isn't it? Her money that keeps 'em in yams and beer? There's one or two working for the Transport now, but they don't take home enough to fill twenty bellies, even at the crazy great wage they're getting nowadays. No, copper, Eve is like a kid with an ant's nest—one of those glass-sided jobs. She knows that if she goes poking round, ordering 'em about, she won't learn much, so she just sits and watches. It's her toy, and she won't let any of the other kids touch it. I met a guy in a pub once, a journalist who was nuts on anthropology, so I told him about the Kus. He wanted to come and set up house here and do a color-supplement piece about them—they're dead photogenic—but Eve warned him off, scared him stiff with libel lawyers and dug up a mossy old friend of her mother's who was his editor's godfather. She was bleeding mean about it; in fact, I could have done with the money and then some. Still, she's had a cruel life, poor old Eve, and it's not fair to hold her responsible for all her actions. Sometimes, copper, I thank God I'm here to look after her. I don't know what would have happened to her without me."

The maudlin note was back, less strong but no less repellent.

"Do you think," said Pibble, "from your knowledge of

them, that one of the Kus was likely to have murdered Aaron?"

"Shouldn't be surprised. He could be a bloody-minded old bastard. Y'see it was in his interest to keep the tribe stagnant, preserved, like one of those mummified Vikings they find in marshes. Then he was somebody—hail to the chief, you know. The moment they seriously tried to fit into the pattern here, get jobs, move about a bit, meet people, he'd be a leftover. I tried to take some of the younger ones out a bit, show 'em life, knock the corners off, but Aaron pretty soon whistled 'em back, with Eve's help. I don't mind telling you, copper, that though I owe the Kus a lot that doesn't mean I've got to like every bleeding one of them. And I wouldn't be surprised if some of the younger ones got frustrated enough to knock the old bastard on the head."

Aha! How did he know that Aaron had been knocked on the head? Had Mrs. Caine said anything about it? Yes, she had. Damn!

"Can you think of any other motive for one of the Kus to kill him? Or anybody else?"

"Not on the spur of the moment, old boy."

"The deceased was clutching a two-headed penny. Does that mean anything to you?"

"Not a thing, copper."

Had there been a pause, a tiny crackle in the self-confident glaze? Pibble knew he wanted to think so and tried to allow for his own prejudice. No, he decided, there had not.

"Are you left- or right-handed, Mr. Caine?"

"Group Captain Caine, if you don't mind, old boy. And I'm as right-handed as they come. Look, my fists are different sizes, even."

He spread his palms out, flat, over his fork. Like a hypnotized hen, Pibble leaned forward and craned down at them. They were big hands with square palms, white and callus-free. The little fingers seemed only half as long as the others. The right hand was visibly larger, and its heart and head lines were joined together in the single horizontal which palmists call the simian line and believe to be a sure sign of criminal degeneracy. Still staring, Pibble wondered whether Walewski had borne the same stigma.

"Seen enough, copper?"

"Yes, thank you."

Pibble straightened up, back onto his ignominious perch, then decided he'd *had* enough and stood upright. Caine did not stir.

"D'you mean," he said, "that the old bastard was killed with a left-hander? That makes it look pretty like a Ku, if you ask me. They always . . ."

"Dr. Ku has already explained the point, and I am bearing it in mind."

"Well, don't strain yourself, copper. So long. I'll be seeing you."

"Thank you, Group Captain, for your help. I'll let myself out."

At the top of the steps Pibble turned right, away from No. 9; right again along the spick-and-span street; right at the lights. Yes (the lost details of the district were coming clear in his mind), there was still a telephone kiosk on the corner of the little square, momentarily unvandalized, too. He rang the Yard and asked for Sergeant Crewe.

"Mike? Jimmy Pibble here. Got a pencil and paper? There are half a dozen things I want checked on. Ready? One: a Professor Fleisch at Melbourne—in the anthropology department, I should think. Anything he can tell me about a New Guinea tribe called the Kus, Dr. Ku who belongs to it, and the sort of circumstances in which one of them might murder their chief. Second: this Dr. Ku got her doctorate in anthro-

pology in roughly 1954, odds are at London University. Find
out how serious a figure she is, and anything useful. Third:
Turner's Hotel, Crerdon Road, Southampton—did one Group
Captain Caine spend last night there? Get on to that one
quickly, Mike, and make sure the people at the hotel realize
this is serious; there's something a bit fishy there—he got back
from Southampton without even a toothbrush. Fourth: ask
Tim Speer whether there's a 1930 two-point-three Alfa
Romeo in London which someone in the trade might have
lent to a pal last week, and whether it'd do a hundred and
twenty. Fifth: ginger Australian Air Force Records into
letting you know all they have about this Caine, missing in
New Guinea during the war, returned to Australia 1946—
might have a police record then—now in England. Sixth: if
Superintendent Rickard is driving home this way this afternoon, ask him if he could spare me five minutes; I'd like his
advice, but it's not very important. Seventh: nor is this, but
see if you can get someone to find out how a place called
Flagg Terrace came to be called that and built like that.
That's the lot—will you read them back? . . . Fine. No, it's
a lucky dip at the moment, about twenty possibles, one a real
swine. I'll ring again before lunch—you might have something
from Southampton by then."

Though it must have been near noon by now, with the
sweet May sun bouncing off the stilted sycamores outside,
all the lights were still on in Dr. Ku's living room. Even so,
it did not seem as staring as it had earlier. Sixteen jet-black
faces, like a platoon in some Zoroastrian skirmish, fought
against the light. They had been waiting for him for some
time, evidently, but with the patience of peasants awaiting
the oppression of the taxgatherer. The furniture had been
moved. A card table and one of the little gilt chairs were
set for him at one end of the room; the sofas had been pushed

against the wall opposite the windows, and seven inscrutable women sat on them in a silent row, all ugly and one horribly misshapen. Eight men stood in a group between the windows —or, rather, two groups, six graybeards and two blackbeards. Paul still sat at his desk, painting with the absorption of a craftsman in the grip of his daemon. Dr. Ku, slim in her Hamlet garb, leaned against the wall behind him.

On the card table were little piles of filing cards, one pile for the women, one for the men, one for Dr. Ku and her Paul, one with a slip of paper on top saying, "Children at school." There was an envelope labeled "Finance," and a note on another piece of paper saying, "None of us would think it an impertinence if you were to refer to us by our given names, including Paul and Eve. There are too many Mr. Kus and Mrs. Kus in the house for formality to result in anything but confusion." The handwriting was very small and square, the letters unconnected.

Pibble sat down, dithery with irrational panic after his meeting with Caine. How in holy hell (unless Fernham and Strong turned up some blood spots in someone's linen basket) was he to cope with picking a winner out of those sixteen un-differentiated and inscrutable faces? Even after twenty-five years, Caine couldn't tell some of them apart, so how was *he* to tell when they were lying, or flanneling, or pulling his leg? And as for motives! He realized that everyone in the room, except Paul, was looking straight at him, one black stare mitigated by Eve's brown-colored eyes. Odd that she was so resolutely not looking at what Paul was doing. Oh well, here goes.

"You all know," he said, "that Aaron Ku, your chief, was killed on the stairs last night. I am here to find his killer. Perhaps that killer came from outside. Perhaps he is one of you. I must make sure. The killing was done an hour before midnight. Did any of you hear anything at that time?"

Silence.

"Do you all understand what I am saying?"

Silence.

Pibble glanced at the top card in the left-hand pile.

"Melchizedek Ku, do you hear what I say?"

"Your tongue is lucid and apt, policeman."

The voice was as deep as Paul's, but grittier. The speaker was second from the right in the group of graybeards, a very fat man but with most of his weight low on his torso, which was thus shaped like an American space capsule. He had a thin tassel of beard, which wobbled as he spoke.

"Then why did you not answer me first time?" said Pibble.

"There is none to speak for us. Our chief is dead."

"I see. Well, then, I am the Queen's servant, and I appoint you, Melchizedek, to speak for the Kus until you choose yourself a new chief. . . ." He'd made a mess of it. The tension and shock in the air were tangible. Plunge in deeper. "And Leah Ku will speak for the women." Tension and shock gone. He wondered if Eve had purposely put the most suitable leaders at the top of the pile; he wouldn't put it beyond her.

"Now, Leah and Melchizedek, are there any of your people who do not understand what I say?"

"The men understand."

"The women understand."

Damn. He must remember to put the men before the women. Leah, he thought, was the beldame who had knelt at Aaron's feet, though it might have been any of the four older ones. Two were obviously younger, and an unfortunately ugly one had strewn the herbs. She clearly had some disease; even in this strong light she seemed hardly to possess a distinct outline, as if she were some figurine which the sculptor had scarcely begun to model before he was called on by a celestial gentleman from Porlock. Funny, Pibble would have expected her eyes to be small and piggy amid those hummocks of flesh, like a whale's. He turned his head away, as an animal abashed, from her soft jet gaze.

"So I may take it that none of you heard anything?" he said.

A deep, formless muttering, like double basses tuning up.

"The men heard nothing."

"The women heard nothing."

"Right. Now the next thing to sort out is whether we can be sure if there are any of you who could not have done the killing. Some of you must sleep in the same rooms, for instance, and could not leave without—"

A knock on the door, and Fernham entered, gripping a boy by the shoulder.

"I found this one, sir, upstairs under a bed, reading with his thumbs in his ears. I think he's just playing truant, sir. And there are several locked doors on both the top two floors, sir. Do you want us to force them?"

"No, thank you, Fernham. That's all for the moment. You've done very well."

Pibble looked at the boy. He might have been any English urban school child in his scrambled-into blazer and flannels, except that his face was as black as a boot. Otherwise it was an English face, beaky and bony, not the squashed, half-melted look of the Kus. He was about fourteen.

"Hello," said Pibble, "where do you fit in?"

"I'm Robin Ku," said the boy. "I'm supposed to be at school, but Jacob and Daniel didn't go to the buses, so I thought I'd lay off, too—it's bloody geography, and I haven't done my homework, and I thought no one would notice. They were all so busy with bodies. And bobbies."

He smiled, confident in his own charm, pleased with his tiny joke. Pibble flicked through the pile of school children's cards. Martha, Luke, Robin, Mark, James, Ruth—surely there wasn't a Robin in the Bible.

"You haven't told me where you fit in," said Pibble.

The boy studied the formal arrangement of people in the room.

"That's my mum." He pointed to the half-formed herb strewer. "But tribe-wise I belong over here." He passed close in front of the card table and settled cross-legged at the feet of the elders, giving them suddenly the look of people posed for a group photograph.

"Right," said Pibble. "Where were we? Um, yes—I was asking whether any of you slept in the same rooms, so that you could know of each other's movements in the night. Melchizedek?"

"The men sleep all in one hut. It is the custom of the Kus."

"And the women, Leah?"

"The women have that custom also."

"I see. That should simplify matters." Should it hell. "But I imagine you are all very silent movers—you could get about so that I could not hear you pass. Would it be possible for one of you to go out of the room where you sleep without any of the others hearing? Melchizedek?"

"Elijah is the keeper of our door."

Elijah's beard was a Hemingway fringe. He was the one in the brown polo-necked jersey and brown corduroys, an arty getup. His voice had the same low register as the other male Kus.

"I sleep at the door, lest some stranger should come in, but I think none could go out, either."

"And the women, Leah?"

"I keep our door. None passed in the night."

"Are none of you married, Melchizedek?"

"We do not go to sleep to beget our children."

He answered deadpan, but the room thundered with deep laughter, delighted female giggles riding the storm of noise. Eve was laughing as happily as anyone. Only Paul worked on in a daze of concentration. The riot ended in a decrescendo of coughs and squeaks. Pibble plugged on.

"Elijah, wouldn't Aaron have disturbed you when he came in?"

"The chief sleeps in his own hut."

"So none of you could have left your rooms last night, except Elijah or Leah themselves?"

"What about Paul and Eve, Mister?" Robin was trying to sound detached and bored, but his voice had not broken long enough ago to keep the squeak of excitement out of the penultimate syllable. He was one who was never going to achieve the midnight timbre of the pure male Ku.

"Thank you for reminding me," said Pibble, and made the mistake of hesitating between sarcasm and avuncularity, like a tennis player trying to convert a drive into a pat in mid-swing. The result was so inane that it was an effort to look at Eve. She rescued him impassively.

"I do not think, Superintendent, that we can prove that we did not commit the murder in concert, but we share a bed so creaky that it would be impossible for either of us to embark on a midnight excursion unknown to the other."

Pibble sorted through the pile of men's cards while the Kus enjoyed their laugh. Really it was like trying to solve a crime in the Stock Exchange, the way the mildest mention of sex interrupted business.

"I see that Jacob and Daniel have jobs with London Transport," he said. "Should they not be working now?"

One of the younger men answered, solemn as a priest at a graveside.

"We cannot leave the Kus until a new chief is found."

"Um," said Pibble, interested to know that the young ones

took their tabus as seriously as the old ones, and wondering whether Robin's cockiness extended to questioning his elders' lore. "That looks as far as we are likely to get for the moment. I think I must tell you that it still seems to me probable that the murder was done by someone who lives in this house, and I must impress on you that it is your duty as citizens to tell me if you know anything which might help me solve the crime. I will question you individually later, but first I must search the locked rooms upstairs. Who has the keys?"

"Elijah has the key to the men's hut," said Melchizedek.

"I have the key to the women's hut," said Leah.

"Constable Fernham told me that several rooms were locked."

"Only two," said Melchizedek. "The walls have been taken away."

"I see," said Pibble. Eve must have spent a packet setting her tribe up in the style to which they were accustomed. "I will search the men's room myself. Leah, I should also like to search the women's room, but if that would offend you I can send for a policewoman to do it."

"Search, Mister. The Reverend Mackenzie taught us that the law is above our customs. I will come with you. There will be matters you do not understand."

"Fine. Well, we'd better get on with it. . . . Oh, just before you go" (casual, now, casual), "have any of you seen a two-headed penny in the house?"

Not a sausage. Pibble had been listening like a hunter. Perhaps there'd been a whisper of indrawn breath in the group of men, but too slight and quick to be sure of, let alone traced. Try again.

"I'd better explain. When Aaron's body was examined, he was found to be clutching a penny in his hand. Not just an ordinary penny"—Pibble scratched some change from his trouser pocket and held a coin up—"with the Queen's head on one side and the seated woman on the other, but a penny with a king's head on both sides. Does anyone know who it belonged to?"

Blank. Blankety-blank, in fact. Where in screaming hell was he going to make even a clip in the featureless façade of this case? Pibble spun the coin fiercely in the air, caught it, and slammed it on the table.

There! Done it, by God! Tension tangible in the room, as if a demon had slid through the door behind his chair. The hair on his nape stirred, but he managed not to look around. One of the elders had opened his mouth like a zany, but no words came before Melchizedek's black claw dug into his shoulder. Paul stopped drawing for the first time, stared at Pibble, and then glanced carefully at Eve, who was watching, with a small frown, the byplay among the men. The women were whispering.

"Well, Melchizedek, what does it mean?"

Silence.

"Why the excitement, man?"

"Policeman, I cannot tell you what a penny with two heads may mean."

"Then what was all the fuss about when I tossed my penny just now?"

Silence.

"Eve?"

"I do not know, Superintendent."

"Paul?"

"Superintendent, I cannot tell you."

A nice distinction, and Melchizedek had used the same ambiguous phrase. Pibble felt that Paul meant him to catch it, and the dark glance that flicked sideways to where the women sat.

"Leah?"

"Rebecca will speak."

The shapeless creature at the farthest end of the sofa began to struggle with language; she was the first inarticulate Ku Pibble had come across, but at once he sensed—or, rather, wanted to sense, wanted to feel—that that peat-water gaze was not a symptom of less than human intelligence, that the impediment was only physical.

"White man come . . . talk with Reverend Mackenzie and . . . Moses and Aaron throw penny. . . . We hide. . . . Yellow men . . . come . . . burn . . . kill."

"This white man, was he Group Captain Caine?"

Nod.

"Moses was the chief?"

Nod.

"You saw Group Captain Caine talk with the Reverend Mackenzie and Moses and Aaron, and then toss a coin. Who else saw this happen?"

"Many."

"Of the people in this room, who saw this happen?"

"Paul . . . Nahum . . . I do not know. . . . More."

"Paul, why . . ."

Oh, let it pass for the moment. Let's assume that Caine had tossed a penny twenty-five years ago to decide something with Eve's dad (presumably), and that shortly after this unfamiliar gesture the whole tribe had been near-as-dammit obliterated. Wouldn't the act of tossing a penny have the same effect of sick shock on the survivors as the echo of a traumatic moment does on any neurotic? Though why had they left it to Rebecca to explain? Presumably Paul hadn't wanted to drag it all out in front of Eve, but the others . . .

And did it matter? Well, it might conceivably have been a (even *the*) two-headed penny which had spun and sung in the tropic clearing. Better slog on.

"Nahum, did you see this?"

"I saw this."

Another graybeard, in a bulging boiler suit this time, and another colossal bass.

"And did you hear what they spoke about?"

"When I was a hunter, I talked no English."

"Did you hear anything, Paul?"

The black mask panned up from the desk, taut with patience.

"I heard nothing, Superintendent."

Pibble caught him, just, before he plunged back into the world he was creating.

"Can you guess?"

"No."

"How soon after Group Captain Caine's arrival in the village did this happen?"

"Two hours, no more. Dr. and Mrs. Mackenzie had fed him in the mission house. I was houseboy. Then Dr. Mackenzie sent me to summon Moses. Aaron came also. They spoke out by the altar. We had no church in the village, but an altar stood in the open before the mission house. Then I saw Caine laugh, and he took a coin from his pocket, tossed it in the air, caught it, and slammed it on the altar, as you did on the table. Then he laughed again, and Dr. Mackenzie led him back to the mission house, still laughing. Hysteria, I now perceive."

"Um. Was it dangerous for you that the Group Captain should stay in your village?"

"Everything was dangerous when the Japanese were in the mountains, but I had heard Dr. Mackenzie and Mrs. Mackenzie talking the day before of a village which had been burnt because they sheltered Australian airmen."

"Thank you, Paul. Melchizedek, do you all know the purpose of tossing a coin?"

"We have seen it on the television set."

"Have you ever seen a two-headed penny used?"

"Two years ago, the bad man tossed a coin to decide whether the white-haired woman must come with him to Berlin to search for her lover, although the bad man well knew that this lover was tied with a rope in a barge near Wapping. But the white-haired woman turned the coin over and saw that it had two heads, and from that she knew the badness of the man, whom she tricked, so that he went to Berlin while she untied the rope that bound her lover."

The Kus sighed and clucked with nostalgic appreciation.

"Did Aaron see this?" said Pibble.

"Aaron saw this."

Pause for thought—excited reverie, rather. Suppose the conversation with Dr. Mackenzie had been about whether it was fair to the Kus for Caine to stay in the village, and suppose Caine had tossed a crook penny to decide, and suppose, all this time after, Aaron had seen this drivel on the telly and (being distrustful of Caine—that we know) had found a chance to nip next door and look for the coin. . . . Steady, steady. How could Caine have known Aaron knew? How could he have got in? Could Mrs. Caine be lying about his being away? Why (an academic point) had the Kus insisted on Rebecca's telling the story first when they all knew? Just because we *want* Caine to be our man it doesn't let us off the rest of the rigmarole. Stop daydreaming; search house. (Anyway, even for Caine, you couldn't call it more than a fractional-motive.)

"Oh well," he said, "thank you very much. I shall have to ask you all to stay here for quite a time yet, while I and my men look through the rest of the house. Perhaps it would be best if we started with Eve and Paul's quarters, and then Leah took us over the women's hut. Then Melchizedek can take us through the men's hut, and then you can all go to your own quarters while we do the rest of the house."

The Kus said nothing, but Eve gave him a minute encouraging nod. Pibble turned and found that Fernham was still in the room, which saved an undignified bellowing for minions down the stairs.

"O.K., Fernham, will you hang on here and keep an eye on things? I think Dr. Ku has a bedroom down here, and I'll try to clear that first."

"Yessir."

Eve's bedroom. A place for sleeping in, a world of taste away from Mrs. Pibble's dainty, pink-frilled, feminine retreat. White walls, no pictures, mannish dressing table, long built-in cupboard, bookcase of Penguins mostly with blue covers, ruddy great brass bedstead with white candlewick cover. Pibble lay gently on the bed, which responded with a thousand twanging instruments. He moved himself a careful half inch, and achieved a rich rococo chord. He rolled right across the snowy expanse and found that the whole bed was mined with noise. Well, it was an alibi of a sort, though he'd hate to have to bring the witness into court. Look through cupboard. Not a skirt in sight, but some brave summer blouses in the drawers and every shade of trousering. Separate section held two blue pin-stripe suits, above drawers with a few white shirts, socks, and underwear—Paul's wardrobe. Tiny bathroom next door, but nothing there; linen basket empty; medicine cupboard Spartan—but ha! folder of contraceptive pills, solving the unaskable question. Rum, Pibble thought, that he should feel distinctly relieved. Nothing hidden in lavatory cistern or any of the other places amateurs always think of. Back to living room.

There were three rooms on the floor above—the one where the body had lain, another small one with a big bed in it (one of the places, presumably, where the Kus didn't go to sleep to beget children), and the women's hut, which Leah unlocked for him.

Walls had been knocked down to make a very big room.

The windows in the far corner were barred, so that section might once have been a nursery. The place was light and clean, not jungly or un-English, not even strange, except for the number of beds in it; rows of modern divans were punctuated by chests of drawers, and three blue cots with transfers of bunnies on the woodwork. With two huge old Victorian wardrobes at either end, the furniture left precious little floor space. The effect was more like a dorm in *Fifth-Form Ballet* or *Martian at St. Monica's* than anything else.

Pibble prowled around. The farthest wall was a partition behind which was a double bathroom and three lavatory cubicles. There were dirty clothes in a container, but no bloodstains. Nothing hidden, either. He came back into the main room.

"Which is your bed, Leah?"

"This by the door. Before I sleep, I move it across, so that none can open the door."

"Why?"

"It is the custom. The men's hut must be tabu to the women, and the women's to the men, lest either defile the other."

"But would anyone want to?"

"By accident, perhaps. We have thought it best to keep what customs we can, so that the Kus remain one together. Without our customs we are lost, we are nothing."

"I thought I saw two of you learning to read."

"You saw that. It is not good if our children have skills that we lack. Moreover, if we are to stay in this land, it is foolish not to read. Moreover, the Reverend Mackenzie would have wished it."

"Are the men learning as well?"

"They are unwilling—they hold more strongly to the customs than the women. We will keep a custom if it agrees with our comfort of living, but the men try to make their lives agree with the customs. They dream of the village, and the days when they were wild Kus in the jungle."

"There are more beds than women, I think."

"The children sleep with us—the girls always, the boys until their balls drop and they are ripe to go to the men."

"Did Aaron want to go back to the village?"

"Half of him wished to go. Half of him wished to stay, because Eve wished it."

"Are you sure of that, if the women and men keep apart so much?"

"Aaron was my husband."

"I'm sorry."

"It is nothing. He is with God. Will you search now?"

It did not take long. All the drawers and cupboards contained clothes. Somebody had an unusual liking for a shade of electric violet. The ritual objects were all together in one drawer—intricately patterned gourds, ultra-chunky necklaces of polished wood and shells, flute-like pipes, and pots of brilliant pigment (make-up for feast days, Leah said). No one seemed to have any possessions of his own except the children, by each of whose beds was a box with two or three toys in it. There was a shelf of battered children's books, too, and a Bible by every bed. The effect on Pibble was of small lives lived bleakly.

"Do you spend all your time here?"

"We sleep and pray here, and those who are unclean stay here for the days of their uncleanness. Most of our life we live in the women's kitchen, or in the senior common room."

Pibble did the double take Graham had hankered for. This black beldame spoke an English as precise as any High Table could desire, but if . . .

"I think it is a joke of Eve's," said Leah. "What you would call the nursery we call the junior common room. It is difficult to know with Eve. He is not like the rest of us."

"No, no, of course not. Do the men use the senior common room as much as the women?"

"When there is television, they come, but at other times they stay in the men's hut. And they come for feast days, naturally."

"Ah. Um. Thank you, Leah. I'd better ask Melchizedek to let me see the men's hut now, I suppose."

Something had happened in Eve's room. The impassive school-photo groups had lost their poise and become a mob, a silent race riot, clustered around Paul's desk. Not quite silent—little grunts and breathings came from them as they jostled for a view. They looked excited but not happy; disturbed, stricken, less than they had been. Paul still sat on his stool, gazing at what he had done, his mouth open but drawn sideways and down as he scratched rakingly at his jawbone. It took him ten seconds to notice Pibble; then he rolled the gray paper up into a cylinder and lunged with it across the desk. Pibble stepped forward and took the scroll as if he'd been receiving the freedom of some city. He returned to his table, sat down, and unrolled his trophy, a blaze of color, done with bright-inked felt pens. It was the wrong way up, so he turned the picture around.

The huts were burning, with crazy, stylized flames. In front of them, the innocents were being massacred. All but two of the innocents were black, the murderers orange. In the foreground, the leader of the orange men watched with his hands in his pockets while two of his soldiers tightened a cord around the neck of a ginger-bearded European in Livingstone-style explorer's kit—puttees, plus-twos, linen Norfolk jacket. A big floppy linen hat lay on the ground and beyond it another orange soldier clawed at the jodhpurs of a woman held supine for him by two of his fellows. Both scenes, uncomplicated by European dress, were echoed several times in the middle distance. Two laughing orange soldiers sprayed a group of running graybeards with their tommy guns. Another was walking stolidly toward the altar, a black baby dangling by the heels from either hand. The spaces between the scenes of action were scattered with an open-work pattern of black bodies, formalized but still agonized. You could see, from the shapes they lay in, that they were dead. Underneath the picture was written in capitals, "IF YOU DO NOT KNOW THIS, YOU KNOW NOTHING OF US."

Pibble stared at the picture, a bit of him saying silently, "Um, yes, I see now"; another bit chilly with shock; and another bit saying, "It really is pretty good stuff by any standards—I wonder what it would fetch." Then he stood up and took the picture back to Paul.

"Thank you."

"Thank you."

Paul opened a drawer, took out a lighter, and flicked it into flame. The gray paper caught at a corner, and the frontier of flame began its invasion across the whole sheet. In the silence, Pibble could hear its tiny roaring. Paul walked to the window and threw the sash up. He held his burning horror out in the open air until the flames closed around his fist. When he let go, an updraft took the last fragment, still flaming, upward past the shorn sycamores and out of sight. Pibble remembered Eve.

She was sitting on the sofa beside Robin, who was beginning to fidget. In a couple of minutes, Pibble realized, he'd think of some way of drawing attention to himself. Eve was as still as ever, except for the huge, slow breaths she was taking. Her face was bloodless, her soft lips blue. She might have been a medium in a trance.

IV

"Goodbye, Mummy. Goodbye, Daddy. Take care of yourselves and don't do anything I wouldn't like."

"Do be careful, darling."

Typical of Mummy to talk as if a month in the jungle with a brood of savages and a sick airman were an enterprise similar to crossing Princes Street. Eve looked hard at her parents, knowing how unobservant and untrustworthy her memory was. Not that she'd ever make a mistake about Daddy's loopy clothes, but in a month she might easily get his face wrong. Very thin, with an absurdly goatlike straggle of ginger beard; the small nose peeling, as always; Wedgwood eyes set rather close, which, with the craning stoop of the scholar-priest, made him look as if he'd just mislaid his pince-nez. All that was easy. Eve tried to learn by rote the high curve of his cheekbones, with a little rubbery muscle just above them; his mouth soft and small. For the first time in her life, she paid attention to his ears, decided they were nondescript, and felt cheated in a way that she did not feel about her failure to fix his huge, elusive personality. That was a long-accepted mystery.

Mummy was easier and harder. No secret about what she was *like*, a sister of Writers to the Signet doing her duty by God and Scotland under uncouth skies. A beauty still, if a little yellow with quinine, but not an unusual beauty; it was only the context and her half-mannish garb, topee and shirts and jodhpurs, that made her spectacular. In Edinburgh, in her own circle, there must be a dozen like her, each coping with making two ounces of butter last a week with the same poise as Mummy had shown last night when Bob got drunk. How was she different, really different, from them? Eve gave up and just stared hard at her in an attempt to use her eye and brain as a camera, even finishing with a fierce blink to copy the closing of the lens shutter.

Daddy said, "One moment," and went back into the hut. He returned with a book.

"I think you might find this useful."

"Oh, Daddy, I *will* take care of it."

"Remember, our people don't have quite the same ideas, but they do have something of the same way of thinking. Give Aaron what help you can."

Eve opened her rucksack and, by stuffing a shirt down the other side, cleared a slot of space into which the book would slide without squashing. Daddy was not a collector of objects, but this was one of his few valued possessions—mostly because it had helped to shape and confirm his life's work, and only marginally for the sake of the signature scrawled across the flyleaf: "Regards, Bruno Malinowski."

"Goodbye, darlings."

She turned, the rucksack swinging heavy in her hand. Bob was waiting, looking pale but larky. He wasn't carrying anything.

"All set to be an egg in the other basket?" he said. "All aboard for Aaron's Ark. Isn't there one called Noah who could have been put in charge?"

"I'm afraid Noah's too old and silly," whispered Eve.

Bob laughed. The rest of the Ark were waiting in a silent, unhappy group, the women carrying more than the men. They filed out of the clearing. Aaron led them along imperceptible hunters' paths. Bob and Eve seemed to be the only ones who made any noise. It was slow going, uphill all the time, and though they'd been marching most of the morning they were still just near enough to hear when the firing started. Eve thought it was a woodpecker before she realized it was an automatic weapon a long way off. Everyone stopped; then Aaron turned off the path into virgin jungle and they worked their way downhill through a screen of creepers, like ants struggling through knitting. At the foot of the slope was a stream, up whose bed Aaron led his party. As they splashed upward again, Bob said, "I hope no one down there knows where we're going. Those Nips know a thing or two about torture."

Eve picked her way among the washed stones and singing water, her mind shuttered against images. She was glad the photograph had not come out.

V

Ah Crippen, thought Pibble, do we really have to exhume this sad old misery? X bashes Y on the nut in the middle of the night, and by midday everyone is beating his breast about something that happened twenty-something years gone by. *I won't have anything to do with it!* Cripes, near as a toucher said that aloud. Anyway, why didn't they *all* nip off into the jungle and hide? Must ask Eve when she comes to. Meanwhile get on with sordid chore of detection.

"Melchizedek, perhaps we could go and look through the men's hut now?"

"As you wish, policeman."

Elijah, evidently, had to come, too. They climbed with the methodical slowness of the old, but with no visible strain. Presumably Aaron had been a bit older still. Pibble could not see that they reacted in any way to the corner where he had been ambushed, or even to the chalk outline that showed the butt and very seamark of the old man's agonized upward crawl. Why up? Wouldn't he have gone down to Eve for help? Skip it. Odds were he didn't know what he was doing in the blind dark, stunned and bloody and dying.

The top landing was slap under the eaves. Only two of the five doors had handles. On one of them was painted a fierce black warrior, holding a painstakingly phallic club—the style the same as that of Paul's big paintings but much cruder in execution. Elijah clawed inside his polo neck and drew out a loop of thong, which he hauled at until a leather wallet popped into view—an effect like that produced by a cormorant when it regurgitates its food for its young. The key was in the wallet. Elijah spat on his right forefinger, drew a line with it athwart the threshold, and then unlocked the door. Pibble went in first.

It was darker even than the stairwell, and it smelled—not the rank, damp smell which permeates the houses of the old and poor and dirty, but a brew richer and just as nasty. Beer, certainly, and a curryish kind of smell, and something else, animal and meaty.

"Is there a light?" he said.

Melchizedek turned and leaned over the banisters to bellow down the stairwell.

"*Falagu kirraputi mili Ishmael.*"

Short pause, then a shout from Fernham below.

"Says they want him up there to light the lamps, sir. Shall I let him come?"

"Send him up."

After a longer pause, the fattest of the elders grunted into view. Without a word, he spat on his finger as Elijah had done, drew the line of the threshold, and went into the gloom. A match scratched and the fat man loomed black and elfish in its small flare. A softer and yellower light steadied in the room and he began to move about with some sort of taper in his hand, coaxing similar flames to light in various alcoves. Pibble went into the room and looked at the first light; it was a homemade candle which gave off yet another un-English smell.

The slope of the roof timbers did make the room very like a hut. Pibble explored, stepping over piles of bedding. There was a lot of space here, doubling back on itself around the other side of the stairwell. It was all subdivided into alcoves, or side chapels, by screens contrived from every kind of material—corrugated asbestos, tin, tea chests, hardboard, softboard, cardboard, old doors, a deck chair, linoleum. Every

paintable surface was covered with pictures in the same style
as the door; mostly they showed men killing animals with
spears and arrows, but some showed men dancing around a
large green snake. No women were portrayed. One of the
alcoves contained large earthenware pots from which the
beer smell came; the biggest was plopping gently to itself. In
other alcoves were what looked like shrines, with carved objects two or three feet high surrounded by what Pibble took
to be offerings: a bent cigarette, a bar of chocolate, pieces of
cloth, wizened apples, a fork, moldy lumps of some doughy
substance, a saucer, a cross of painted sticks. The largest side
chapel contained logs of old wood—no, slit-drums. Pibble
only just resisted the urge to slap one and see how it sounded;
instead he got out his pencil torch and made sure nothing was
hidden inside the instruments. A proper room, cut off at the
far end, held a shower and a lavatory and was fairly clean.
At least there was daylight there; the windows in the rest of
the area had all been blanked off with squares of cardboard.

Pibble walked back toward the door between the patches
of soft, useless light. He ran his pencil torch along the roof
beam. Aha, there was a perfectly good socket with a cable
running along the rooftree; he traced it down to a switch by
the door, and went out onto the landing.

"Fernham!" he shouted.

"Yessir!" came the bellow from two floors down.

"Send someone up with a couple of hundred-watt bulbs.
Dr. Ku must have some to spare."

"Yessir!"

After a longish pause, up scrambled Robin with the bulbs.
His gesture at the door was quite different, a sort of flowing
figure-of-eight movement, made as perfunctorily as the genu-
flection of a guide in a cathedral.

"Can you find me a chair, please, Robin?"

The boy skipped along the landing to the other door with

a handle and came back with a light wickerwork affair, only remembering to slouch for the last few paces.

The room looked quite different under the unshaded glare of electricity—smaller, less secret, pathetic. The ramshackle screens were like a deserted stage set. The shrines shrank and lost their meaning, becoming patterns of litter. Pibble carried the chair down the room, found another socket, and achieved another blaze of desecration. Some of the paintings retained a coarse vigor; some even gained, now that you could see how fierce and improbable the colors were, how fanciful the use of irregularities of surface, how obscene (particularly in the green-snake dances) the detail. The rolls of bedding, too, became more exotic, revealing themselves as not just collections of blankets but a giant's scrap basket of unwanted materials: tattered old curtains, imperially colored; froths of mauve lacework; deep sea-green tablecloths; a kaross; shawls; an eczematous tiger skin. The heaps were quite neat, confined to definite territories, and each accompanied by a wicker basket full of clothes and a cardboard carton of other belongings. Apart from these containers and the mounds of cloth, there was nowhere in the room to hide anything.

Robin had disappeared, back to his book presumably, but the three elders stood just inside the doorway. The Electricity Board had not managed to diminish their primeval blackness one jot. They stood very still, not turning their heads at all to watch him, following him with their eyes. This stillness, combined with their unnatural shortness and breadth (standing together, the three of them formed a compact rectangle of flesh, much wider than it was high), made them seem more alien than ever; not creatures of this earth at all, but invaders from Alpha Centauri. Pibble wondered whether their remoteness was the result of a conscious effort, whether they were exercising some sort of group hypnotism to shove him and his electric-light blasphemies away, out of their private world, banished. If so, he wasn't having any of it. He strolled over.

"Melchizedek, I must search the bedding and clothes and those boxes. Is there anything that you would rather I did not touch?"

"Search where you must, policeman."

Pibble worked down the room, shaking out all the bedding and carefully scanning each side. A splash of blood, unnoticed in the dark of the stairs, might have transferred itself from the murderer's clothes to his bed. (Pibble didn't have much faith in this idea, actually; it seemed improbable that anyone would take the risk of waking the others to sneak about in the dark murdering elderly chiefs.) The beds were neat and quite fresh. So were the clothes. The cardboard boxes all contained one very sharp knife, tobacco, and a collection of inexplicable knickknacks. It took him a good twenty minutes to work around the room, and he didn't find anything.

He stopped at last by the beer-smelling jars.

"What's this stuff, Melchizedek?" he called.

"This is *kava*, policeman. We buy beer at the pub and add our own things to it. It is not the same as the *kava* we made in our village, but it performs what we require. First it makes us happy and then it makes us sleep."

"Sleep?"

"Sleep, policeman. Our bones are old and rub on each other at the joints. Therefore we go in turn to the doctor and tell him that we cannot sleep, and he prescribes tablets for us. These we add to the *kava*, and sleep as we did when we were young men."

Pibble felt like wringing Sandy Graham's neck. First you establish that the murderer couldn't have come from this room because he would have waked somebody up. Then you establish that he wouldn't wake anybody because the others were all in the arms of their barbiturate Morpheus; the murderer might even have added an extra couple of pills to the mixture, supposing the thing had been premeditated. Pibble stared at the floor as he thought. It was a good floor. Typical of whoever built the place that the boards in the attic fitted as tightly as the parquet in the drawing room. Not that one, though. . . . Pibble knelt and scrabbled at the corner of the plank with his fingernails, then with the screwdriver gadget on his penknife. About two feet of floorboard came up. Marvelous thing, the trained eye. In the cavity were a number of pillboxes labeled "Mr. Ku: take two at bedtime"; packets and tins containing herbs, yeast, and unidentifiable powders; a jar of brown sugar and two wooden spoons.

The trained eye then found three more such hidey holes. The first was empty; the second contained a store of do-it-yourself candles; the third, about eight feet from the door and a bit to one side of one of the shrine alcoves, held a yellow bowl with liquid in it and a cloth in the liquid. This was where the meaty smell came from. Pibble knew it well, now he was so close to it. He had last met it as strong as this in a smart little flat off Kensington High Street, where a stock-jobber had gone berserk and sliced his sister-in-law into bits in the spare bedroom—about what she deserved, having been living there rent-free for two years, most of which she'd spent interfering with his life. Silly bitch, she wouldn't have been pleased to know that her blood smelled exactly the same as the blood of the blackest sort of black man Pibble had ever seen.

"What is this, Melchizedek?"

"The bowl we use for making our *kava*. The rest we do not know."

The voice came from straight above Pibble's head, and he looked up. Dear God, but they moved quietly. The three had closed around the hole, so that he was hemmed in by squatly foreshortened torsos which seemed to lean over him, threatening to fall and crush him like buildings in some early German film. He hurried to his feet and felt safer.

"What you call 'the rest,' " he said, "is a mixture of water and blood, with a shirt in it. Whose shirt is it?"

"How should we know? We have many shirts like that."

True. It was a gray ex-R.A.F. job. There had been at least one like it in each of the baskets, and some of the men downstairs had been wearing others.

"Ishmael," said Pibble, "I must stay here. Would you be kind enough to go and tell one of the policemen that I want him?"

The fat man strutted away.

"Did neither of you notice the smell?" said Pibble. "I smelled it myself when I came in, and I understand that the Kus have a very keen sense of smell."

"We smelled it," said Melchizedek. "When you were gone, we would have looked to see."

"But didn't you smell it earlier today?"

Pause.

"I think, policeman, that when a man wakes, the air that has been in his nose all night seems to him good air."

Yes, possibly. He was still looking for another question when Strong came thudding up the stairs.

"Will you please go round to the phone box and get on the blower to the lab people," Pibble said to him. "I want the photographer again, and someone to take a sample of blood. Then you'd better go and get your lunch, so that you can relieve Fernham."

"O.K., sir. I've got a list for you—I'll leave it with Fernham."

"Fine," said Pibble. "Off you go. Elijah, would you please lock the door? No, wait a bit. Are there any more loose floorboards like that?"

"You found them all. You are a fine policeman. Ishmael

laid me three to one that you would not find any, so I am
three shillings richer."

Prompt to his cue, Ishmael heaved his Bunter-like figure
up the final flight, and the three old men embarked on an
elaborate exchange of threepenny bits. Very cozy, thought
Pibble, very calculated to reassure one that they were really
human, man-in-the-street punters, despite the nasty foreign-
ness and incantatory atmosphere of the men's hut. Too cozy?
Phony? A nicely judged piece of improvised harmlessness,
arranged to comfort him? Sometimes you meet a stage Irish-
man who turns out to be real Irish, right to the green marrow;
or a military chap with long, yawning vowels who really was
born in the Punjab and used to play polo with the Duke of
Gloucester. Could be so with this lot; remember to ask Eve
how much they gambled.

He thought of the missing question.

"How do you choose your new chief?"

"We do it by shouting," said Melchizedek. "All the men
gather in the hut and—"

"No," said Elijah. "That is when the wish of the old chief
is known. This time we must use the thrown sticks to—"

"The sticks?" shouted Ishmael. "When the slayer is not
known? You forget that . . ."

"I forget? *Karavlu! Inakai disudu! Damada ni . . .*"

"*Salaboni kani kara kalata firindi nun . . .*"

"*Kalata givariju pim! Sola danu ni goparigoru lava . . .*"

Pibble felt like a man trapped in a bell tower during a triple
bob major. The colossal voices cannonaded at each other,
resonant with echoes from cave-like lungs. Even thus must
the Early Fathers have disputed the nature of the Trinity,
beards jutting, noses six inches apart, face muscles bunched
with passion—except that those holy men had not been the
color and texture of squash balls. At least it seemed unlikely
that anyone had done the murder because he was certain of

inheriting the chieftainship. Constable Fernham came belting up the stairs, truncheon out, a one-man riot squad. Pibble gave him the thumbs up and he halted, panting. The theological bellowings rumbled into silence, like thunder over far hills, and the elders turned to face Pibble. Melchizedek shrugged.

"We must ask Eve," he said. "He will know how we choose a new chief."

"Degrading," muttered Ishmael. "Degrading."

"I suppose that was Aaron's room," said Pibble, pointing at the door from which Robin had fetched the chair. He watched Elijah take a tobacco tin from his pocket and extract a pinch of dust, which he scattered on the threshold and rubbed in with his foot. The ritual of locking, with the key and the wallet and the leather thong, took place as before; then they all went down the landing and peered into the dead chief's room.

It was like a little girl's night nursery, with sprigged roses on the wallpaper and a white-painted iron bedstead. There was even a religious picture on the wall above the pillow, only it wasn't "All Things Bright and Beautiful" but one of Paul's creations, in the style of the burning village, an elaborate Crucifixion. The attitudes of the figures were deliberately stilted, but it was quite clear who was who. In the center were grouped the apostles and the disciples and the Mother of God, and above them the Christ in agony. All these were orange men. The outer circle was soldiers, onlookers, officials, priests, and above them the two tortured thieves. All these were black, as black as squash balls. Pibble felt outraged. He had been conned. How would he ever know now whether the thing got its force because he'd only just seen Paul's other picture, the massacre of the innocents? Or whether there really was a mastering power inherent in this one, absolute? His body gave a shuddering jerk, the sort of nervous spasm it produced every night just as he was dropping off to sleep. He turned to see what effect the picture had on the three elders—or perhaps they were used to it?

But they had gone, gliding away in silence, and were just then floating down the stairs. Pibble went back into Aaron's room. There were a few clothes in the chest of drawers and an illustrated *Life of Jesus* on the table by the bed; otherwise nothing. No loose boards, either. He sat on the bed and thought.

If the blood in the bowl is Aaron's, it means that one of the men did the killing, drugged the *kava* O.K. first, but panicked when he got himself bloodied and tried to clean his shirt instead of cutting it into little bits and flushing it down the lavatory. *But* he must have got himself well and truly bloodied to produce a brew as thick as that, and only on the shirt, too. Don't like it.

The coin, then. Only a coincidence that Aaron had picked that very night to discover that Caine had fiddled the toss twenty years back? Or perhaps he had known since the telly program—the one with the white-haired woman in Wapping—and now was going to use his knowledge in a way which didn't suit the killer: to stop whatever it was that was going on in the hut, possibly; the old boys certainly seemed to have lapsed a bit from the level of Christianity set by Aaron and the women, even on the principle of minimum conversion which Eve's dad seemed to have specialized in. Best ask Robin what's up; he seems bit more detached from the Ku viewpoint than the others.

Anyway, next thing, obviously, is to take the men separately and work on them. Perhaps ask Eve for a bit of guidance first about what they could have been . . .

European feet thudded on the stairs. Pibble went out to the landing, expecting Fernham with news of some domestic tangle caused by his delay, but it was Ned Rickard. Ned had been having a busy time of it lately, by all accounts, and tiredness gave an extra dimension to his woman's-serial handsomeness.

"Hello, Jimmy," he said. "I got a message and came winging. I've got thirty-six hours off, and I'm going to spend it asleep, but I can spare you five minutes."

"Hell, Ned, I'm not sure it's relevant now. I'm sorry you've been bothered. Still, as you're here, there's just a couple of things."

He stopped on the way down to talk with Fernham.

"You can let 'em out now, Constable," he said, "but the men mustn't use their hut until the lab boys have been. In case I miss them, Elijah has the key and there's a bowl of blood and water between the joists there, with a shirt in it. I want the bowl and the cavity printed, samples of the liquid taken, and the shirt gone over for anything relevant. I want the amount of liquid measured, too, so that we know how much blood—someone's sure to ask. Got that?"

"Yessir."

Out into the noon of May. The sun's heat had an edge to it now. Someone was cooking a curry, with garlic. A pretty little girl with black pigtails was writing "DIRTY" in the dust on the boot of Rickard's rusty old Consul convertible. Pibble led him across to the far pavement and turned to face No. 9.

"You see that open window," he said, "slap above the porch. It's on the second half landing, actually. Supposing a competent rock-climber wanted to get across to it from the same window in Number eight, could he do it and how long would it take him? I'm not talking about a thief, a pro—just an amateur who happened to be a rock-climber."

Rickard tilted his beautiful profile to one side and pulled his blue-black forelock. Pibble tried to imagine himself spread-eagled and hurrying across that ornate façade. A chill center of nerves twitched into life in his palms. At least there'd be plenty of plumbing to hold on to.

"Two minutes, average," said Rickard. "If you'd had time to practice, or didn't care what risks you took, you might cut it down to a minute and a half. Minute and a quarter, even, if you were bloody good."

"If you had all the time in the world, would it be easy or difficult?"

"All depends on what risks you took. If that overflow pipe there—the one to the left of your window and a couple of feet above it—would take your weight, it'd be easy. From here I shouldn't fancy it. I'd go the long way round, up to where that waste pipe crosses the big vent pipe. Then you'd have an easy bit along that cornice and a slightly ticklish traverse to the rain-water pipe, and down that. You'd have to be fair to take it that way. What sort of chappie have you in mind?"

"Sizable bastard—come and have a look at him. That's the other thing I wanted you for, and to tell me what is wrong with this picture."

"What picture?"

"The one I'm going to show you."

The archway into Cora Lynn did contain empty bottles now, two speckless ones waiting tidily for the United Dairies man. The door was open, so Pibble led the way along the painstakingly cheerful passage and put his head into the kitchen. Mrs. Caine was sitting very straight in an upright chair by the table, staring at one of the Goods and Chattels posters; she looked as if she were doing some sort of religious exercise.

"May we come in?" said Pibble.

The round head flicked toward them, tiny teeth bared, the quick reflex of the vixen alarmed in her lair. She answered in a whisper.

"Shh! Bob's asleep—he's had a hard— What are *you* doing here, Ned?"

"You've met Superintendent Rickard, then?" said Pibble, filling the foolish silence with foolish words. Ned was looking ill now, not just tired, with a bright circular patch of red in the hollow below his cheekbone and a fine dew of sweat along his upper lip.

"How've you been keeping, Sukie?" he said.

"Pretty well, 'cept that I'm getting fat. That's marriage for you."

"How's Bob?"

"Tired as hell. He's persuaded himself that there's a big future in some sort of Swedish industrial filter and he's got the agency for it and won't let up. And you look like a left-over kipper, Ned. Couldn't you come and have a meal with us one evening?"

"I'd love to, Sukie, but it'll have to wait. I spend all my evenings tailing the exploiters of your sex round Soho. I must go and have a quick nap before this evening's session, if you'll forgive me."

"Can I ring you at your office, Ned? You can't ring me 'cause they won't let us have a telephone."

"Any time. If I'm not in, leave a message with Sergeant Burnaby."

"Goodbye, Ned. Love to your mum."

"Bye, Sukie."

Ned left. Bloody revolting hell, thought Pibble, why is life such a mess? And the tidier bits of it look, the messier they turn out to be.

"I'll be off, too, Mrs. Caine," he said. "I only thought of something else I wanted to ask your husband, but it can wait."

"Shall I get him to come and look for you at Eve's when he wakes up?"

"That'd be fine. If I'm not there, one of the uniformed men will know where I am."

"Goodbye, then, Superintendent. Make Ned get some sleep —he looks *awful*."

There was a stench of blue exhaust behind Ned's terrible

old car. He was revving it rhythmically to a particular pitch of vibration which made the silencer clatter against the chassis frame, filling the enclosed terrace with the mindless pain of a sick machine. Pibble opened the near-side door and slid in.

"Oh Lord," he said, "I'm sorry about that, Ned. How could I have known? Anyway, it doesn't look now as if Caine had anything to do with it; if you'll run me round the corner to the phone box, I'll ring Mike Crewe and with a bit of luck he'll be able to wipe them clean off the sheet. But if he can't I could use another five minutes of your slumber time. You aren't really on tonight, are you?"

"No."

"O.K. You turn right and right again at the lights."

There was something wrong with the clutch, too, but Ned didn't seem to bother that the first few yards were an L-plate judder. The phone box was occupied by two late-teen girls, one dark and one mousy, with greasy white make-up and stringy hair, who were taking turns giggling into the mouthpiece. Pibble rapped on the glass and pressed his warrant card against it. The giggling stopped and the dark girl said something to the mousy one. They looked up and down the street, conferred, and started to dial. Pibble knew the dial numbers in his sleep. . . . There was another knock on the glass. Ned was standing smiling and making a get-out-of-it gesture with his thumb. They came out of it, giggling again, and Pibble went in. The receiver was still off the hook.

"Are you there, caller? This is New Scotland Yard, 230 1212. Are you—"

"Extension 458, please," said Pibble. He'd never got through as quickly on his own—nor would those fool girls if it had been a real emergency. "Mike? Jimmy Pibble here. Any luck with any of that stuff this morning?"

"You were right about that Southampton doss house, sir. He uses it as a kind of social alibi, low-grade Bunburying.

The proprietress says he's a nice gentleman with a jealous wife, but she doesn't want to keep anything from the police. He's been doing it for several years now, but he hasn't been there for a month. Superintendent Speer's in Essex, but I got on to a guy I know who put me on to another guy who says he'd bet his life there hasn't been a two-point-three Alfa in the trade for several weeks, and it would have a top speed of a hundred and ten, and a casual borrower who took it up above ninety wouldn't get lent a car again. Nothing from Melbourne yet, of course, or Australian Air Records (they'll take *months*), and London University's being standoffish but I've an appointment to see someone this afternoon. I left a message for Superintendent Rickard and I've found a policewoman in traffic control who's a whiz on London history. Sounds as if they've landed you with a beaut this time, sir. Anything else I can do?"

"No, thanks, Mike. That's fine. I'll be in for an hour tomorrow morning, and if you can get the Coren file tidied up by then I'll buy you a box of Black Magic. I've got Superintendent Rickard here now, and I want to let him go home for a spot of kip."

"Needs it, I do hear. So long, sir."

Ned was back in his car, but hadn't started its neurotic clattering again. He just sat staring at the backs of his hands as they rested on the bars of the steering wheel; his face was collapsed and grayish, with blue tints in it, wicked and old. Pibble got into the passenger seat and found it hard to look at him.

"I'm sorry, Ned," he said. "It's a grisly coincidence. I wish I'd known."

"Not your fault, but there aren't as many rock-climbers as all that and there was a fair chance I'd at least have been acquainted with her. And him, I suppose. Is he in the clear now?"

" 'Fraid not. He told me he spent last night at some hotel in Southampton, and he didn't. Otherwise he's got half a motive and no opportunity, unless Mrs. Caine lied. Would she?"

"Yes."

"Um. Presumably he could have done that climb we were looking at in the Terrace."

"Bob? Not on your life. He'd never have got out of the window. He's lost his nerve."

"But I thought he was something of a tiger. That was the other thing I wanted to ask you about. I saw a photo of him in what looked like a crazily dangerous position, and—"

"I know that one. I saw Sukie take it. He's about six feet off the ground."

"Um. How well do you know him?"

"As well as I know anyone, except my mum. Better than he knows himself—a lot better. I've got a file on him sixty pages thick, *and* he stole Sukie from me."

"If you've got that much on him, you must have known where he lived."

"Yes. I'm sorry, Jimmy. I was play-acting. I had to take the chance to see her. I couldn't do it off my own bat, you see. I didn't push you, did I? I waited for you to take me?"

"Sure. Tell me about Caine."

"I'm not a good witness. I'm not even sure I'm sane about him. But I'll tell you at the start that I'm sure he hasn't the guts to bash someone himself. He'd wheedle someone into doing it for him, *and* they'd think he was doing them a favor. Anyway, I first met him in the Salisbury. You remember when Dick Gurney caved in and I had to take over the whole Furlough shemozzle? I found a note among Dick's papers about this Johnny who specialized in picking up would-be actresses and nudging them into the Furlough machine. Furlough has a line in very high-class girls who have clients in influential positions (that's another complication; you'd be surprised), and there's a lot of wastage. Some of 'em can't stand the pace and lose their looks; some of 'em get ideas which don't suit Furlough; some of 'em marry; a few of 'em even become actresses after all. Anyway, they're always looking for fresh talent, and employ the odd callous charmers to bring it in, on a piecework basis. I thought I'd have a look at this guy and make out that I'd like to be taken on in the same sort of capacity. Odds were I wouldn't get far, but the Furlough boys wouldn't know my face and there was just a chance. A nibble here, a nibble there, and one day . . . Christ, I'd like to mash them into bleeding pulp. Anyway, I hit it off pretty well with this guy; he's the kind who can make you feel happy and clever simply because he's bothering to pay attention to you. I talked about climbing, because it was nice innocuous ground, and it turned out he'd been out in Nepal with Standring and had had a vicious time of it getting back after the avalanche, and now he hadn't the nerve for it any longer."

"Was that true?"

Ned was silent for twenty seconds. Then he said, "I don't know. I never thought to check up. Standring's lot were all Australians, so we wouldn't have come across them over here. It shows you. Bob's like that. You remember how Dick Gurney had a habit of inventing villains out of harmless citizens? Well, I wanted to like Bob and to think Dick had been up a gum tree, so I said why didn't he come down to Wales one weekend and see how he felt about a bit of simple rockwork? I suppose I thought that if he *was* a villain I might get a useful cross bearing on him. Sukie came, too, of course, and that was that."

"Just like that, in one weekend?"

"Just like that. He can do it, you know, just like there've always been women who can do it to men. He's very useful to Furlough, though I hear whispers that all isn't quite cozy. Bob must be a weakish point in an organization as tight as that, and I have a hunch that he's broken their rules a couple of times and had a warning that there'll be really nasty trouble next time. Anyway, he took Sukie from me in three days, not trying at all, as far as I noticed. And *she* isn't a feather-headed flibbertigibbet, either. She's a real tough egg, and one of the best climbers I'll ever meet. You know what it is makes a real climber, Jim? Not nerve, or strength, or the sort of thing you see on gym displays on the telly, though they're all useful in their way. It's the knack of getting every particle of strength into a single muscle movement—hooking a couple of fingers into a cranny—but keeping your mind, your *will*, in a state of intense balance so that the immediate physical focus is only a part of what's going on. Otherwise you find yourself screaming with cramp a good five yards before the next possible resting place. Sukie's a natural. If there were vertical races in the Olympics, she'd be climbing for England and all the papers calling her a golden girl, instead of which she's married to a ponce and cooking tagliatelli in a basement. She *can* cook, too."

Pibble sat silent for a while, thinking of the balanced will which knew exactly where each pepper pot was in its kitchen. Yes, that'd be useful if you were reaching for a fissure hundreds of feet up and an inch's uncertainty might mean that you became a sprawling lump of meat on the screes below. Her husband must be an encumbrance, too. He saw, for a second, Blondin wheeling a top-hatted Edwardian across Niagara.

"When did you change sides?" he asked. "About Caine?"

"Ach, it's a long story. Bob hung around at the foot of the climbs making sensible remarks, then strolled up by sheep paths to meet us at the top. Has it ever struck you that rock-climbing is the purest of all sports, Jim? There's hardly a worthwhile climb in Europe which my mum couldn't see the start and finish of, walking up by the easy way. No cups, no quarrels with coaches, no interviews with flash journalists (unless you've got a color supplement to sponsor you)—you just hang there and reach for your next hold. Anyway, one way and another Bob spent a good deal of time with us, talking deprecatingly about Standring and making no bones about having lost his head for heights. That's how Sukie came to take that picture. It was after supper, which accounts for the horizontal shadows, and we'd all been drinking a bit. Somebody was teasing Bob and he was holding his own, of course, but Sukie came over all defensive (I should've realized then) and swore that he was a better man than any of us. Honestly, I don't think I started it—I was still on his side— but a bit of needle got into the conversation and the upshot was Bob said he'd take us up to the Monk's Corner and show us just how badly his nerve had gone. So we all trooped off— there's not much to amuse one at that time of night on top of a saddle in mid-Wales—and up Bob started. He'd draped himself with all the paraphernalia; he's got a feeling for things like that—put him into the Middle Ages and he'd wear his hauberk as if he'd been born in it. The Monk starts easy and gets quite severe, but it's interesting the whole way. You know, there are climbs which are difficult but somehow *dim;* you do them and go somewhere else. But if you're in those parts you make a point of doing the Monk, however often you've done it before, so Bob must have seen quite a few of us starting up the first ten feet, which is like a ladder, almost. There was this large light falling yellow from the west, and Bob walked up to the rock and went whistling up the first few feet. Then, yards before he was in any trouble, he looked back over his shoulder and laughed aloud and said he couldn't go on. That's when Sukie took the picture."

"I'll save you the rest, Ned. You had to come back Sunday,

but Caine and your Sukie decided to stay down for another day when the rocks would be less crowded."

"Yeah. Sukie was in a lull between hospitals; I hitched a lift, and left them the Consul to come back in. You're a knowing old bastard."

Rickard banged the side of his fist on the horn button. The unoffending and patient vehicle gave a startled *peep* and Rickard blinked and switched the ignition off.

"When did you decide that Caine was really a villain?"

"Difficult. I started my file in November, but I'd been pretty well certain for weeks before that. Still, I didn't want to know it. O.K., he'd pinched Sukie from me, but I was— am—fond of the kid and I didn't like the idea she'd turfed me out for a creep. The worst man winning is bad for morale, you know. I don't say I felt—feel—Sukie had any moral duty to prefer me to him, but there are limits; besides, I don't want her to muck up her marvelous youth—she's the kind who's got a duty to be happy. Still, I told Burnaby to keep an eye on him, not saying why. We've got quite a machine, you know, and it wasn't difficult to log his appearances in the relevant pubs and clubs, and keep track of who he was with and who he talked to. At first I persuaded myself he was an innocent out for kicks who'd had the bad luck to meet up with a nasty lot. Still, I didn't fancy warning him off myself, so I thought I'd have a word with one of the girls. She's dead now, took an overdose last Christmas Eve, left a note saying she couldn't face the tedium of Christmas dinner with the family. That's why I picked her; she was loopy about the truth. Diana Hazard, born Chloe Maggott, always told her clients her real name before she even took a stocking off. Anyone else would have faked something a bit more melodramatic by way of a suicide note. Not a whore with a heart of gold, mind you—meaner-hearted than most, in fact —but a truth addict. She told me about Bob."

"Which side was she on?"

"Neutral. She wasn't the kind who likes or dislikes people, but she respected him as a professional. He had this talent and he used it in a way Chloe understood and with an efficiency she admired. I couldn't go on persuading myself Bob was an innocent after listening to Chloe."

"When did he find out you were a copper?"

"I think he knew all along. He's fantastically perceptive about people. I bet he knows more about *you*—about what goes on inside you, anyway—than I do, Jim. I think that's part of the reason why he picked on Sukie—a nice, savage, unanswerable way of riling a copper. He may even have been simple enough to believe it'd muck things up for me if ever I pinned something on him—look like personal malice. He wouldn't have considered what Furlough would think about it—he's not at all clever, you know, quite incapable of thinking three minutes into the consequences of any of his actions. He's the sort who shuts his eyes and hopes the nasty consequences will go away and bother somebody else. Look, Jim, I'm not going to sleep much after this, anyway—at least not till I've taken some sort of action. Let me just nip back and root around among my gang—I might be able to find out what Bob was up to last night. Burnaby's made something of a hobby of him and he was out till midnight, so there's a good chance he'll come up with something. I'll be back about three."

Pibble looked at him. He was still porridge-colored with fatigue, but no longer tinged with the hectic pallor of a dying Keats; and his voice had gathered from somewhere a little of its proper fizz and bounce. Pibble wondered whether to tell him that the whole Caine imbroglio looked like being academic now that he'd nosed out a basin of blood. Ah hell, he *wants* to go, poor fish, and it did seem an uncanny amount of blood. Explore every avenue, if only for the pleasure of telling defense counsel that you've done so.

"Thanks, Ned; that would tidy things up. I'll cushion Mrs. Caine as far as I can."

"Cushion yourself, you sentimental old weasel. Sukie's quite . . . But it's a kind thought. So long."

The Consul jerked away, the rattle of its muffler nagging the afternoon air. Pibble realized that his stomach was calling, softly but insistently, for its ritual sausages and cheese and bitter. That would be beautiful: an hour in a quiet corner with the *Guardian* crossword puzzle; sixty sacred minutes free from the fury and the mire of human blood. Still, nobody digests happily on a dicey conscience. Better nip back to No. 9 to say where one's off to, and check whether the lab people have come. Besides, Fernham had Strong's *Good Pub Guide.*

The lab men were grouped around the hole in the floor, in a blaze of photo floodlight. They glanced at him, frowning, artists disturbed in mid-creation; they looked like an early, small-screen TV play, with the whole cast crammed into five feet of stage. Pibble craned over shoulders and saw that they'd hardly begun on fingerprinting. Fine, plenty of time for lunch. He recognized the pathology man, young and spotty but not stupid, but couldn't remember his name—something odd about it. Pibble edged around the group to him.

"Care to guess how much of that is blood?"

"No, sir. Not yet."

"Shame on you, Thackerey." (Got it; he spelt it with an extra "e.") "Professional reticence at your age! Suppose I were to lay you three to one that it was more than a teaspoonful and less than a pint, would you take me?"

"One to three against? Twenty to one on, more like. No, sir, if you're thinking in those terms, the wise money will be going somewhere round about half a cupful, and getting about five to one on it."

"Thank you. If you're right, it seems a lot to come squirting out of the back of a bashed head. D'you know yet which group the old boy was?"

"Yes, sir. O."

"Fat lot of use that is."

"Yes, sir. Bad luck, sir."

Pibble craned again. The fingerprints were visible now, gray on the yellow enamel of the bowl. They looked improbably thin and delicate, like a woman's. Pibble went downstairs and Eve met him on the first landing, carrying a blue loose-leaf folder and a little packet of filing cards.

"I have some reading matter here for you," she said in her most prissily academic accents; he was sure now that they were a symptom of stress or embarrassment. "You may care to occupy yourself with it over luncheon. Paul is quite right; you cannot understand us without some knowledge of our past. But I think if you concentrate on the moment of obliteration you are likely to achieve a wrong emphasis. I could lend you the books I have written, but that picture would also be partial, because for academic reasons I have minimized the part played by my father. The best I can do is this."

She shoved the fat folder at him with an uncharacteristically gawky gesture, and continued.

"It is several attempts to write a biography of him, none of them at all successful, but in your peculiar circumstances you may find it more illuminating than a finished work. I lack altogether Paul's bent for summoning whole areas of experience into a single temporal framework. Minute particulars are more my line."

She laughed her Edinburgh teatime laugh, but went on less regally.

"These are the cards I got out for you, and the note on our financial affairs. You will keep them confidential, won't you?"

"Of course."

Pibble flipped through the cards and found the one he wanted. The information was there but meant nothing to him.

"What is monotro'aic melanemia?" he said.

"It's a very rare hereditary blood disease, found only in New Guinea. With proper treatment, especially diet, it has no effect at all, but in the wrong circumstances it can affect the nerve centers and the processes of growth, with the results you saw in Rebecca. She's been like that since she was twelve. My father tried to persuade her mother to feed her the right things, but he was very averse to overriding anyone. It doesn't affect her intelligence at all; she was the first of the adults to learn to read."

"That's what I felt. Another thing, if you've got the time, how will the Kus choose themselves a new chief?"

"Normally they would do it by acclamation, because the dying chief would have made his wishes known. Failing that, there's a kind of eeny-meeny-miney-mo method, involving the throwing of ritual sticks on the ground, but they certainly can't use that if there's a possibility of Aaron's killer being chosen. Otherwise there's a prolonged but very interesting ceremony which consists of elaborate competitive boasting about each man's prowess and possessions. They take it in turn and each contender has to raise the previous one, as in a poker game, by making a bigger boast and by placing an object of greater value than the last in a central pool. In the end, contenders drop out, either because they are bankrupt or because they've used up all their boasts, and the bravest and richest man becomes chief. He takes the pool, but he has to redistribute it among the tribe without keeping noticeably more than he put in. He can do this any way he likes, and can thus bind key figures in the tribe to him."

"It sounds like a potted version of a Republican Party

convention," said Pibble. "Are you eligible yourself?"

"I would be if I broke off my relationship with Paul and took a wife. So would Paul, of course, which was what Aaron really wanted, though I don't imagine he talked to anyone except me about it."

"At least it sounds as if nobody can have been motivated by a certainty that he would succeed to the chieftainship."

"No. Is that all?"

"For the moment, thank you very much. Do you know where either of the uniformed constables is?"

"I think Mr. Fernham's in the men's kitchen—it's on the right in the basement."

"Did you have to put kitchens in when you came?"

"Three. There's a little one for Paul and me. The Gas Board thought I was pulling its leg."

"I can imagine it."

In the basement, the smells were outlandish and hungry-making, though the doors were shut. All the men were in their kitchen, the three young ones working carefully through Kempton Park runners, four of the elders playing knucklebones on a deal table, and a fifth stirring a very big new saucepan on a gas cooker. Fernham was slouched against the wall, helmet off, pretending to watch the game but really staring at the cook. This was a Ku whose Christian name Pibble had not yet identified, but whom he had mentally called The Poacher because of the jacket he wore, an elaborately pocketed and flapped affair in a green dogtooth tweed. It might have been made for some large and jovial squire, but on its present owner it hung below the knees. As Pibble watched, The Poacher groped in a pocket and withdrew a pawful of small brown paper bags which he smelled in turn before putting a couple of pinches from one of them into the brew. He put the bags back and began to search another pocket; this took some time, but at last he pulled out some small black objects (spiders?) and popped them in, too. Pibble crossed to Fernham.

"Smells good," he said. "D'you know what it's called?"

One of the knucklebone players, Elijah, glanced up.

"We call it stew," he said.

He picked up the bones in his right hand, flipped them into the air, caught four on the back of the hand, slid them off into a small pile, picked up the fallen two, tossed them a couple of feet into the air, picked up the pile, and caught the two as they fell. He seemed almost to have time to wait for them to come down. Then he did the same with his left hand. The black limbs moved so fast over the bleached deal that they lost their outline, becoming a patterned flicker like leaf shadow.

"Strong left this for you, sir," said Constable Fernham.

Pibble read the list. There were eight pubs on it, with the name of the brewer followed by three columns of figures, which turned out to be points awarded for food, clientele, and comfort. The Station Hotel had far and away the best score; its brewer was down as "Bass, but careful landlord" and there was a further note: "It's all right once you're inside."

"Thanks," said Pibble. "If anyone wants me, I'll be at the Station Hotel till about two."

When he got there, Pibble found he knew it well, a crazy adventure in turreted brick, a fistful of Mouse Towers, an abandoned design by Ludwig of Bavaria, the whole loutish hodgepodge shouldering out toward the roaring roundabout where the Ring Road crossed the A-something. (Not Pibble's idea of a pub, which was a back-street nook kept by a silent old man who lived for the quality of his draught beer. It would be empty when Pibble used it, except for two genial dotards playing dominoes, but its finances and its bitter would be kept healthy by squads of thirsty men working in a trade so peculiar that they had to do all their drinking at hours when Pibble was dredging for torsos.) Pibble willed his stomach to pessimism and went in.

The Bass was beautiful; the cheese was strong Canadian cheddar and the sausages Harris, cooked to a mahogany fatness; the butter was butter. Pibble, as he settled down to read, wondered why Strong wasn't farther up the ladder. If he had served his job as he had served his superior officer . . .

The cards turned out disappointing, collections of bony fact which Pibble couldn't put flesh on. The old men were a bit younger than they looked: Aaron had been fifty-eight, Melchizedek was fifty-four. Everyone seemed to be related: Leah was Ishmael's sister, Elijah was . . . Ach! Hell. He'd take them home and he and Mrs. Pibble could spend the evening constructing a genealogical table; that might amuse her for a bit.

The sheet of paper labeled "Finance" read:

I inherited a considerable amount of property from my mother, whose mother's father had been a successful speculative builder in the middle of the last century. This has enabled me to bring the Kus here and to maintain them—not as expensive as it sounds, as we prefer to live frugally, except for heating. Simon, Jacob, Daniel, and Magdalene work for London Transport and bring home roughly £50 a week between them. Paul's earnings from his paintings vary considerably, but recently he has been doing very well, earning just under £2,000 in the last financial year.

All this, together with most of the income from my property, goes into the Trust which I have established for the benefit of the Kus. Dr. Kerway, of King's College, London, and myself are the surviving Trustees; Aaron was one.

I pay a pension to my old nanny, whose name I do not imagine to be germane, and I have left her a sum of money in my will.

I have no relatives, according to a firm of detectives I employed to ascertain whether any existed. I have left Paul enough money to maintain him should his talent fail. The rest will go to the Trust.

I have not told any of the Kus, except Paul and Aaron, about these arrangements. The men would regard it as an impertinence on my part and the women as not being their affair.

Aaron himself had no property beyond a few personal possessions. These would be valueless, except for the Crucifixion Paul painted for him, whose value (as it is not quite in the style of the paintings which have been selling so well) is difficult to estimate.

Clear, thought Pibble, but beside the point. I wish she'd put down how much rent Caine pays and whether he pays it. And whether the Kus are conscious of the extent to which she is supporting them. Can they guess how much her glass-sided ants' nest is costing her? Are they even aware of the value of money? They must be, after all that telly. And what . . . Ah, forget it. He turned to the chunk of filial piety in the blue loose-leaf folder.

It was not a coherent document. As far as Pibble could see, there were three distinct beginnings, about seven different swatches of middle (some overlapping), and no ends. Several title pages were scattered through all this, none apparently connected with any of the parts. One said, "*The Reverend John Hennekey Mackenzie, A Memoir*"; another, "*The Guinea Stamp*, by Eve Mackenzie"; and another, "*After the Manner of Men, An Experiment in Anthropology*, by Dr. Eve Ku."

There was a genealogical table on a different size of paper and with different typewriting—the work of that detective agency, presumably. They'd done their stuff, going back three generations all along the line and more elsewhere. Eve's mother's mother's father, the note on finance had said; the table made him Ephraim Flagg, builder, *d*. 1893, leaving two *d*., one unmarried. A thoroughly unsatisfying solution to *that* mystery. Perhaps it meant that Eve owned the whole damned Terrace—say five flats in each of eleven houses, let at an average of four guineas a week (you couldn't visualize her as the extortionate landlord beloved of journalists), and not all that much upkeep on buildings put up by the proud and virtuous Grandfather Flagg. (Pibble stopped to wonder whether Eve knew anything about him; surely he must have left legends behind, to people the turrets of his fantasy.) Say ten thousand quid a year before tax, probably more. How many of the Kus would the tax hawks let her list as dependents? Rebecca, perhaps; Robin and the other kids? Bob Caine? Tchah!

He smothered his last morsel of bread with mustard, balanced a carefully preserved triangle of cheese on top, and began to read, chewing. She seemed to have tried every known style of biography:

. . . In many ways a typical child of the Manse. From that source he drew his romantic but practical venturesomeness, his deep natural piety, his belief in the virtue of labour, his obstinate certainty of the rightness of his own motives. But from what fey Celtic strain did this typical Lowlander inherit the visionary side of his faith? His almost Oriental ability to accept both of two conflicting truths? His uncondescending sympathy with alien modes of thought and action, so far from typical of the Lowland Scot? His spiritual humility? His . . .

There were several pages of that, with every abstract noun balanced by a contradictory one and hardly a fact anywhere.

School in the village was not like school elsewhere. Attendance was not compulsory. Adults and children both came, the women and girls and small boys squatting on the floor on one side of the big hut, the men and youths on the other. Down the gang-way between the sexes Mackenzie walked. No writing was attempted. Mackenzie argued that it was more useful and less disturbing to the pupils if he worked on the resources of their elaborate oral culture, the (to a European) incredible memories, and the ingrained desire to arrange the structure of facts and events into ritual patterns. When his daughter came out at the age of thirteen, she joined the class, but was lost without these special abilities and had to have coaching in the evening.

A typical class sounded like a long, rambling, bilingual con-versation. Mackenzie insisted, with some justice, that each party was really teaching the other, since he was learning (slowly but to an extraordinary depth) the habits and thought patterns of the Kus. It is one of the tragedies of modern anthropology that his early death prevented his knowledge from being set down on paper. What a substructure it would have provided for the ob-servations and theories of his more superficial colleagues!

He spoke to his class in both English and Ku, but never in any sort of mixture. He despised pidgin English, declaring that it was a tool of colonialism and the badge of a subject race. Instead he taught, with considerable success, standard English. He repeated longish passages in English and Ku, relying on the memory of his pupils to retain the one while hearing and com-paring it with the other. After slow beginnings, this proved wholly successful.

Pibble skipped an intricate analysis of the areas of the two cultures with which the language of the other did not overlap, and picked up again where a capital "C" caught his eye.

But what of his avowed purpose in being in New Guinea at all, that of being a Christian missionary? Here again both his beliefs and his methods were personal and eclectic; and perhaps he was fortunate that the Church of Scotland maintained no organized missionary structure in New Guinea; his superiors would have been unlikely to approve of all he did. He felt that the more closely Christianity could be integrated with the existing customs of the Kus, the better. Dr. Schroeder, Baptist colleague who worked in a group of villages a dozen miles down the valley, used to twit him by saying that Mackenzie would have condoned head-hunting—had that been a custom of the Kus—as perfectly consistent with Christianity. Mackenzie would laugh and say his was the only way he could work. The basis of his every action was solid and abiding respect for each individual man, with a conviction that man's existing structure of beliefs was a part of his being, and therefore a part of human civilization. Uproot these beliefs, with however creditable a motive, replace them with however noble a creed, and your converts will be half destroyed in the process of conversion, at best dependent and at worst demoralized. And, in the end, the old roots will send out suckers, draining the strength from your new graft, corrupting and killing it. The last state of your flock shall be worse than the first!

Pibble skimmed again, this time an unconvincing and, he thought, unconvinced discussion of the nature of conversion. It had the feel of a conversation heard long ago and imperfectly remembered. He next found himself in the middle of a section, apparently earlier in date, written horribly in the historic present.

John walks slowly across the great patch of beaten earth between the huts. The whole tribe is assembled to see him, men and boys in one group, women and children in the other. Between them stands the chief and behind him squats the priest with the ceremonial slit-drums. The Kus believe that this priest, jealous of a rival, brought sickness and death to John's predecessor by incantations, drumming, and a magical arrangement of sacred bones. The previous missionary died, in fact, of malaria, but the priest is a creature of power. John speaks formally to the chief, asking permission to live among them. He exchanges a careful greeting with the priest and . . .

A hand fell on Pibble's shoulder, blighting his repose, an

accent of lead. He knew who it was without looking up, and before the voice spoke.

"What'll you have, copper? Another pint of ordinary? They know how to look after it here."

Caine picked up Pibble's tankard and strode off to the bar, his steps artificially long and masterful. There was a fair-sized group of lounging shouters there, but he was through it and being served at once. Angrily Pibble fished two and tuppence out of his pocket; he didn't want another pint, however good. But at least he did have something he wanted to talk to Caine about. The man came back, slopping beer without apology over another drinker's suède shoes.

"I'm afraid," Pibble said, "you'll have to let me pay for my own. We must keep this talk on a formal basis."

He slid the coins across. Caine said nothing for a full ten seconds; then he put the beer down.

"Bad as that, is it?"

"You told me you spent last night at Turner's Hotel, Crerdon Road, Southampton. The hotel informs us that they have in the past provided you with an alibi for social reasons, but that you were not there last night. They are not prepared, you see, to give false information to the police in a matter of importance."

Caine laughed happily, and his eyes crinkled at the corners as though he had suddenly begun to enjoy himself.

"Poor old Ma Gittory," he said. "Must have turned her blue rinse green getting mixed up with the cops again after all these years. You shouldn't have done that to her, copper."

"It was hardly we who did it. I will now ask you again where you spent last night."

"Honestly, old man, I'd rather not."

This wasn't going to be any good. The light but candid voice, the smiling eyes, the lasciviously rueful curve of the lips—all declared that Caine had decided to tease him and wanted him to know it. In a spasm of schoolboy temper, he said the meanest thing that came into his mind.

"Never mind; we'll find her ourselves quite easily."

Crippen! Had he scored, or was Caine just sulky because he wasn't going to play the game? Anyway, he replied in the tone of a cheat discovered.

"Are you implying, copper, that my marriage is less perfect than it appears?"

"If it is, you may be sure we will keep the fact to ourselves."

Caine picked up his glass and crossed to the telephone on the far wall. He found sixpence, dialed, listened for a long time, hung up. Started to dial again and stopped. Finished his beer standing and moved toward the door. Pibble beckoned him back with a sideways nod of the head. Caine hesitated, then came.

"Another thing I'd like to know," said Pibble. "Was there a priest in the village when you were there? I don't mean a Christian priest—a pagan, or whatever you'd call the religion the Kus had before Mr. Mackenzie turned up."

"I was bloody sick most of the time, so it's not much use asking me. But there was an old boy who blew flutes with his nose during church. They didn't have proper hymns, 'Father, Hear the Prayer We Offer,' and that caper—just a sort of wailing and thumping and some of them danced. I thought it was blasphemous, but the Rev. swore it was O.K. And this flute figure was different from the others. He had scars all over him, done on purpose, in a pattern, not just the three on the face like the ordinary men had. And they all acted very respectful with him. None of the usual cackling and joshing. I gathered he'd been some sort of holy man. That what you want?"

"Yes, thank you."

"So long, then."

Caine left. Pibble went to the telephone and dialed the Yard. Ned was out but he got on to Sergeant Burnaby.

"Afternoon, Burnaby. Has Superintendent Rickard told you about my troubles? Well, look, I've just tackled my chap about it and I don't think he's going to be any use to me, but he might be to you. He was with some woman last night, and he tried to ring her up (I think) and got no answer, and then he started to dial someone else and thought better of it. He overacted quite a bit, so I think it's possible that he stepped out of line last night (he's done it before, Rickard says) and is scared of Furlough finding out that we're badgering him. Anyway, I'd bet my boots there's something a little fishy there which might give you a bone to gnaw at. So if you can get a line on the girl . . . You have? Crippen, that's a bit of luck! Ned told me you'd made a hobby of him. . . . I'd like to have a word with her if you can spare her. . . . Oh, O.K., I'll go gently. She'd better not come right to the house, though. Can you get her to the Station Hotel out here before closing time? Looks as if there's a little bar round on the west side. I'll go and have a word with an estate agent while I'm waiting; there's one with a funny name just by the railway bridge, if you want me."

Well, Pibble decided, you deserved the occasional fluke, even if it was more likely to add its pebble to the cairn of evidence that would one day send Furlough down than to get him—Pibble—much further with his excursion into anthropology. Quite right, too. Pibble thought he'd like to hear the argument about capital punishment as a deterrent applied to a case like this.

In the fumy air of the main road, he began to wish he'd had more of his second pint. He could easily sit and wait for Caine's bird and do his neglected crossword puzzle. Will power won, just.

The estate agent was nothing like as seedy as he'd remem-

bered, but the name was unaltered—Lackadaisy, Lackadaisy
& Squill, all freshly picked out in gilt paint. The "For Sale"
notices were written with an electric typewriter on paper
with an ultra-classy heading. Freeholds from £15,000 up;
flats at 20 gns. a week and more, suit young executive. Pibble's
money-counting soul gasped at a photograph of Brissac
Street, a fag end of long lease going for a mere £6,000. He
wondered whether that was the house where he'd gone to
pick up a sixteen-year-old pilferer and found him singing a
sick baby to sleep in a room with half a dozen other kids
littered about, father snoring on the bed, and mother weeping
into the parsnip stew on the gas ring.

In the front office, a weaselly youth glanced unimpressed
at his warrant card and disappeared, returning almost at once
to say that Mr. Evans-Evans would be glad to help him. The
further office was small but rich, with a thick dark carpet, a
vast desk, and one of Paul's paintings over the fireplace. Mr.
Evans-Evans was wearing a Magdalene tie and a tiny, tidy
beard. He stood up and shook hands with Pibble across the
desk; they had to stretch a bit to achieve contact, like house-
wives in those medieval cantilevered houses demonstrating
their ability to shake hands across the street from their upstairs
windows.

"Well, Superintendent, what can we do for you?"

"I don't really know," said Pibble, "but it might help me a
bit if you could tell me something about property values in
this area. *Your* firm seems to have looked up quite a bit, for
instance. I knew it just after the war."

Mr. Evans-Evans deprecated with an eyebrow, and began
to speak very rapidly but just distinctly enough to understand,
in the manner of a priest rattling through some prayer for
minor members of the Royal Family.

"It is hardly the same firm, you know, we are really an
old established West End partnership but a dozen years ago

I had a hunch that this was going to prove a lively area, much livelier than any of the local chaps realized, it was only just beginning then, of course, so I persuaded my father to buy out Mr. Josset, you may have known him, big reddish chap and rather demoralized after a lifetime of arranging leases on slums, so here we are and very lively it's been."

He paused for a long draught of breath. Pibble had been looking at Paul's picture, which was in his best-selling style and showed a marmalade tomcat stalking through a blue-green pattern, very jungly. There was a bird in the cat's stomach, lying on its back with its wings crossed in the attitude of pious resignation in which undertakers lay out the dead. For all the formalization of style, this cat was a particular cat, very smug and feline, not at all anthropomorphized.

"I take it you've had some dealings with the Kus?" said Pibble.

"You like it?" said Mr. Evans-Evans. "I didn't at first but I took the advice of a cousin who has a flair for that sort of thing and he swore it was bound to appreciate over the next ten years, that was before Kus became O.K., so I dare say he's right already, but now I've got used to it and you'd have to offer me a very good price indeed to tempt me to sell, can't say more than that, can I?" Gulp of breath. "I take it you're the officer concerned with this bizarre mishap at Flagg Terrace?"

"Yes," said Pibble. "I really want to know what the whole property is worth today, and whether you think it likely that any pressures have been put on Dr. Ku to sell."

Mr. Evans-Evans sat down behind the desk, opened a drawer, took out a pair of spectacles with rims like fortifications, put them on, and changed his personality. He began to speak in a slow, light, precise voice.

"Let me see. I must first decide how much it is proper for me to tell you, because I am more deeply involved in the matter than you may realize. Let me deal with your first question, since that is straightforward enough. The value of Flagg Terrace would depend on what the buyer proposed to do with the properties. Suppose he were to keep them as they stand, get rid of most of the existing tenants (you may be aware that Dr. Ku does not ask an economic rent for her flats), and spend some thousands on modernization, he could derive an income between twenty and thirty thousand pounds a year from them. That would include a selling price of around two hundred thousand pounds."

Mr. Evans-Evans took off his spectacles and added a parenthetical mutter: "That is supposing you could find tenants with that sort of money who were prepared to live in a terrace that looked like that, it's not what people expect these days, nothing you could do to it would ever get it into *House & Garden*." He put his spectacles on again.

"But that would be an improbable solution. I do not know if you realize how much ground Flagg Terrace covers with its gardens. If the buyer were to pull down the existing houses, he could erect nearly forty new dwellings and sell them at up to thirty thousand pounds apiece, thus realizing his profit in three or four years instead of waiting for it to dribble in over the decades, with unpredictable governments always likely to deprive him of it.

"I think it would be in everyone's best interests if I were to, ah, 'come clean' over the second section of your inquiry, at least in general terms. I myself was asked by a certain syndicate to put 'feelers' out about this very property. They would certainly, with the Borough Council currently in office, have been given planning permission and were proposing to erect a group of neo-Georgian houses and maisonettes which they considered tasteful. I have since learned that another syndicate, who on previous form would have built something more modernistic, was also interested. Furthermore, there is a rumor that Sir Cyril Blight is looking for a place somewhere in this area to put up one of his tower blocks. You see, the beauty of this particular property is that, though undeveloped, it all belongs to a single owner who shows no sign of wanting to develop it herself. There would be no messing around with unpredictable venders. Furthermore, the new owners could appeal to a Rents Tribunal and get a substantial rise on the rents which the present tenants are paying, so that most of them would have to leave. I promise you, Superintendent, that Flagg Terrace is a real plum. Dr. Ku could dispose of it for a very substantial sum indeed."

"Wouldn't those houses take a lot of knocking down?" said Pibble.

"They are, indeed, wastefully well built, but modern machinery would dispose of them soon enough. That would not add appreciably to the cost."

"Did you talk to anyone besides Dr. Ku?"

Mr. Evans-Evans took off his spectacles again.

"You see," he said, "the first time I went I tried to appear primarily interested in the painting and I just threw in the odd remark about the property, so I was a bit taken aback when Dr. Ku took me up on it at once and asked me to come back when she had what she called her Trustees available. I got a sort of impression that I'd mentioned a subject which had already been discussed and on which Dr. Ku wanted to have the facts clear, so I was perhaps a little over-optimistic about the prospects when I went back. You fish."

The last two words were absolutely unmodulated, so it was a second or two before Pibble realized that he had been asked a question. He shook his head, and the thin dribble of words began again.

"Very sensible of you, seeing what a boring sort of pastime it is, mostly, and not economically justifiable by any means, but it has its moments when you see a slight change in the surface and color of the water, you feel it as much as you see it, really, and you know there's a big one there and the question now is can you get him out. That's what I felt about Flagg Terrace the morning I walked along there, it's a mistake to go in a car to that sort of meeting, makes the whole thing seem too important at the start, but I was singing 'Land of Hope and Glory' under my breath, I remember."

Mr. Evans-Evans glanced down at his spectacles with a shy half smile, as if apologizing to them for such a childishly uneconomic use of the air. He put them on and was at once back in the world where the Lackadaisys and the Squills collect sevenpence-halfpenny off every pound that changes hands.

"We met in Dr. Ku's room. Dr. Ku was there herself, with a Dr. Kerway and Mr. Aaron Ku. The last was a colored gentleman, inappropriately dressed for a meeting of that nature. Paul Ku was not present, but I heard someone practicing a stringed instrument in the adjacent room."

Pibble remembered the musical bed.

"Dr. Ku informed me that the three in the room were the Trustees. I cannot imagine what a chancery judge would think of this Trust, but apparently it exists for the benefit of what Dr. Ku called the 'tribe,' which appeared to mean the rest of the household, and the Trustees administer it. However, the property itself appears to belong solely to Dr. Ku. She told me that if the Trustees wished to make arrangements which affected the way of life of the rest of the tribe, the men at least would have to be consulted. There was a strong suggestion from Mr. Aaron Ku that this would be something of a formality.

"I outlined my position, with the natural reservations. I did not say more than if they wanted to sell I might be able to find someone who wanted to buy. Then Mr. Aaron Ku asked straightforward questions about the amounts of money likely to be involved, which I answered by saying that they would be fairly substantial but that I could not commit myself further. He made a distinct effort to pin me down, but I refused to allow him to. Then Dr. Ku asked about the existing tenants. That is customary. Most venders wish to make a show of concern but can easily be satisfied with generalities. Dr. Ku, however, was particularly insistent, and I had to outline the true position with greater clarity than I had intended. Dr. Kerway, who is a lecturer at London University, said very little beyond making unwelcome attempts to clarify particular phrases I had used. He seemed decidedly less businesslike than the other two, but even so I found it a peculiarly tricky interview. In the end, Dr. Ku said that they were glad of my help and would get in touch with me if they came to any decision. Dr. Kerway said, 'Really it's up to you, Eve,' which seemed to displease her. She then thanked me again for coming and I left. That was fourteen months ago."

Mr. Evans-Evans took off his spectacles with a flourish and shut them in their drawer, indicating quite clearly that the interview was over. Pibble rose, but Mr. Evans-Evans stayed where he was.

"Really very interesting character, Dr. Ku," he murmured, "very *grande dame* in an odd sort of way, had an odd sort of life, I suppose, but underneath they're all the same, these gracious ladies, we see quite a few of them in our West End branch, of course, all relying on money being power but pretending not to know it, which is what makes 'em gracious, I suppose. Dr. Ku's just the same, really, only her pretenses are a bit more sophisticated, thank you for coming, I'd be glad to know if anything happens that affects my interests, of course."

Mr. Evans-Evans rose and Pibble prepared for the straining handshake across the vast desk. But the estate agent made the long detour around and opened the door himself; his farewell gave Pibble the impression that he was expected to prove, in some mysterious way, an excellent investment. Strong was waiting on the pavement outside, coughing in the indigo murk from the exhaust of a passing furniture van.

"D'you want his number?" said Pibble.

"Thank you, sir," said Strong, "but it's hardly worth it, we've decided. You could keep two men busy all week in this road alone, taking down numbers and prosecuting, and all you'd get is a slight thinning—be able to see the far pavement sometimes—but it'd be back to normal the minute you let up. Fifteen years' time some boffin will be able to write a nice little monograph on the incidence of lung cancer among constables on regular traffic duty. I've got a young lady for you, sir."

"That's kind of you."

"I've put her in a different bar from the one you said, sir. There's a boisterous element goes in there. Hope you liked it, sir."

"Just right, thanks. Know if there's anything from the lab yet?"

"Only a telephone call to say the prints on the bowl aren't any of the ones we took this morning, sir."

"Oho! Wait a moment, though. Bet you they're young Robin's. Or one of the other kids'. Perhaps I ought to— Never mind. I'll see Miss What's-'er-name first."

"Hermitage, sir. Nancy Hermitage, but I don't know if that's her real name. You can't ever tell with them."

Pibble felt oddly uninterested in the possibility of the prints being Robin's; uninterested, too, in meeting a tart who, Burnaby said, had some very influential acquaintances, a genuine *poule de luxe*, apparently. His lust to nail Caine was unsettling the whole case, besides being irresponsible, inefficient, and immoral. And if he did succeed he wasn't going to enjoy himself much in the witness box; they were bound to get on to Ned Rickard's relationship with nice little Mrs. Caine. And what about *her*, anyway? How would that sharp princess take to being rescued from her adored and loathsome worm?

Strong led him to a door that didn't look like part of the pub at all and stopped just inside.

"That's her, sir," he said, "under the Etty."

Etty had not been on his best form during the composition of the work in question. A nude brunette lay face down on a rock below a waterfall, dangling the tips of her fingers in the pool. She was illuminated by a shaft of sunlight between branches, and, judging by the deathlike pearliness of her flesh tones, she was going to be nastily sunburnt if she lay there much longer. Her buttocks were slightly in the wrong place, but it was not obvious how they could be re-sited for the better. Below the picture sat a very beautiful woman in an orange shift.

"O.K.," said Pibble. "Nip back to Flagg Terrace, Strong, and arrange to have Robin's prints taken. I'll be about twenty minutes. Is it really an Etty?"

"Yessir. The private rooms upstairs are full of 'em. This used to be the showpiece pub of the local brewery, but they went bankrupt because the chairman insisted on buying Ettys at the top of the market. What about the other kids, sir?"

"They're all at school, but you'd better arrange for them to be done when they get home. I don't want any fuss, though."

"See what I can manage, sir. Bye."

She wasn't drinking but was using her time of waiting to do her nails with colorless varnish. She looked about twenty-five, a little plump, dark-haired, serene. The two or three male drinkers at the bar moved and spoke with a jerky self-consciousness, constrained by her attraction. Pibble walked over.

"Miss Hermitage?"

"That's me. Are you the policeman they've brought me to see?"

"I'm Superintendent Pibble. Can I get you a drink?"

"No, thank you. Is Bob in trouble? They want to know where he was last night. He was with me."

Pibble wondered if she could put that antique line over as effectively to a jury. She'd be a hell of a witness to have against you, with that husky, assured voice and those kitten eyes.

"How long have you known Group Captain Caine, Miss Hermitage?"

She smiled—a nanny's smile indulging the peccadillo of a favored tot.

"Long enough to know he was never more than Flight Sergeant. But does it matter? The point is he really was with me all last night."

"It matters in a way," said Pibble. "You see, if you were emotionally involved with him you might be prepared to say that whether it was true or not. The more I know of your relationship, the more chance I have of assessing your truthfulness."

"You mean the longer I've known him the more chance there is I'll realize what a sod he is and . . . Or are you just taking the chance to warn me against him? Thanks for the thought."

She smiled again, a courteous dismissal of Pibble's good offices. Then she sighed.

"You realize I'm in a dicey position, Superintendent? I can't afford to go into the witness box. Two or three of my best friends would have to leave me at the first hint of publicity, and most of the others would be very unhappy. And Mr.— my agent would not like it at all. So naturally I'd prefer to wash my hands of Bob and say I hadn't seen him for a week. There's another thing, too; we spent last night in a flat which my agent sometimes lets me use but which really is part of his other business. He'd be angry if he knew we'd used it as a—well, as an ordinary love nest. I'd be O.K. for the time being—I'm a valuable property—but he'd chalk it up against me for the future. He's that sort. But Bob would . . . Well, I happen to know my agent told him about a year ago that if he didn't marry and settle down like a respectable citizen he'd be for it. My agent can be very unpleasant indeed; and I'm sure he'd feel the same about Bob using his flat. So neither of us would want that to come out, and you might think I'd be better off, at any rate, if I kept my mouth shut and let Bob stew.

"The trouble is, I owe Bob a lot. He gave me my start, you might say. I'd never have been any sort of an actress, never got further than I was—two-line parts bought by sleeping with an angel. But I've got somewhere now. I've lots of rich and famous friends, and some of them will still be my friends when I'm a dreary old bag. I make a lot of money, too. My agent takes a big slice but he still leaves me plenty, and he really does look after me—a bodyguard on call if he thinks I might need one, pesterers frightened off, that sort of thing. I'm right at the top of my profession, you might say, and with care I'll stay there for another ten years and then set myself up in a tidy little house in the Cotswolds with twenty cats. But if it hadn't been for Bob I'd still be a part-time harlot with a room in Kilburn.

"So I've got to do what I can for the bastard, you see. Not risk my neck, or even my job for him, but just try and persuade you that if anything happened last night it couldn't have been Bob. I'm not what you called 'emotionally involved' with him, not any more, and I certainly don't go in for the golden-hearted tart line. You don't meet them in real life, you know, 'cept as broken old bags doing it in doorways at five bob a go; they haven't got the detachment. I once went to a flick with one of my friends who's a dear old lady Teddy bear of a Sea Lord, and it was a story about a gallant captain and a golden-hearted tart and he sat there snorting at the sea bits and I sat there snorting at the shore bits and all at once we realized what we were both doing and started to laugh so loud the manager came to chuck us out—only he'd been on one of Snooty's (that's my Sea Lord) ships, the manager had, and he recognized him so we went off to his office and drank Cointreau out of tumblers and Snooty and I acted the film for the manager and the boilerman and some gash usherettes till Snooty had one of his attacks and I had to take him home. Where was I?"

"About Bob Caine," said Pibble, wondering how long his mouth had been open. "Why did you see him last night? It can't have been in the way of business for either of you."

"Ah, it was just a coincidence. My date didn't show up—he'd had to fly off and arbitrate on something in South America, a boundary dispute between Chile and somewhere—so I went off to hang around in a pub where my agent can get hold of me. I don't take on casual ringers-up, or anything like that, but he likes to know where I am. I was feeling a bit off-color because I'd been looking forward to my date—he makes such whacky jokes and he tells me what's going on and who's bitching who in the Cabinet. Anyway, Bob was there—fishing, you might say, and not having any luck—so after a bit I took him off to the Steak House and bought him a meal and we wept on each other's shoulders. He's a sod, Bob, but he does listen to what you say and he makes you feel real and clever and comfortable—it's a con trick, really, but it works—so after a bit I cheered up. But I can't afford to be under an obligation to anyone, even Bob—you'd never know when he mightn't want payment—so I thought I'd cheer *him* up, only he joshed me into taking him to my agent's flat (I've got a key) instead of my own. I don't know why, except that he knew he wasn't supposed to and he doesn't like the idea that anyone can order him about."

Silence. Would she go on unprompted? Once people get into the swing of confession, they'll tell you more than they need, including, possibly, a crumb or two that might actually be useful. No luck this time.

"And what were Bob's own troubles, Miss Hermitage?"

The kitten eyes became a cat's; the creamy skin tautened; the soft lips hardened efficiently into a defensive smile (as presumably they often had to).

"You'll have to ask . . ."

Then the smile went easy.

"And a fat lot of good that'd do you. If lies were loaves, Bob would be in the Joe Lyons class."

"Provided all his loaves rose," said Pibble. "Miss Hermitage, before I met you I was warned that you had friends who could come down hard on me if I treated you nastily. But I'm leaving the force before long, and in the meanwhile I could be very nasty indeed. I could arrange to have Furlough badgered a bit, in a way that made it clear the connection was through you. Or I could see that you were watched in an obtrusive way when you were out with some of your influential friends. But I don't think it'll be necessary, if you'll listen to me. First, I believe you (and even if I didn't, I know that there isn't a jury in London that would agree with me). Second, it's clear that Caine can't have done this killing. Third, *his* life, and indirectly yours, is going to be disrupted until the thing is cleared up. Fourth, there's a good chance that the motive had something to do with him. Fifth, as you say, he's a liar but not intelligent enough to know if his lies are worth while."

She sighed lightly, like a nun regretting the wickedness of the world outside her convent walls.

"I expect you would, too," she said. "Men are absolutely

ruthless. And I wouldn't, of course. I think I *could* get you sacked, if I went about it right, but it would spoil everything afterward. My friends aren't the sort who like to be used like that, even if I managed to make it seem the right thing for them to do. Oh hell!

"The thing about Bob is that he's an idealist. Not the ordinary sort, but he's never come to terms with the world he's got to live in. He tries to live in a perfect world where he doesn't do anything which he doesn't want to do and he knows rich and famous people and women are always there when he wants them and not when he doesn't and there's always enough money and nobody shoves him about. I told you Mr. Furlough made him marry and settle down; he was furious about that at the time, but he's dead scared of Mr. Furlough and quite right, too. Mr. Furlough's got it in for him, I think; he wants to see him come a cropper, I don't know why; Bob does affect a few people that way. Anyway, Bob did what he was told—he'd always had this flat, apparently, but he'd lived in and out of it like a wolf and his lair, and now he found a nice little wife somewhere and she made him all cozy and crawled round worshiping him and he decided he liked the new setup after all. Then along comes a black man and upsets the whole thing. I didn't understand this part, because the black man isn't Bob's landlord but he's trying to make the landlord sell the house, and if that happens the odds are Bob will get turfed out and never get another flat at the sort of rent he can pay. There's something screwy there; in fact, I'm not sure he pays *any*. Then he'd be in real trouble. Mr. Furlough has been longing for an excuse to have him— ach, I won't go into it. *You* know. I don't really understand why his wife can't pay the rent, but Bob says she hasn't any money either, though her father's an admiral and my Sea Lord is as rich as Croesus. I'll tell you a funny thing: I haven't met her but I bet it's a happy marriage. I can smell them; I'm good at that. He'd leave her, of course, if he did get turfed out. Probably he'd get tight and beat her up first —he did that to one of my friends. He likes to travel free, you see, with no baggage wished on him by his past. But I'll tell you another thing: I bet you Mrs. Bob knows a good deal more about him than he realizes—he's lied all his life but he's never got good at it, not once you know him. Anyway, Bob's got to beat this black man by hook or by crook and hang on where he is, and he really sounded rather desperate—for him, that is. And honestly that's all I can tell you. It doesn't sound much, but it took him ages to get round to it. He has this fantasy bit about how he's in charge of the situation, the strong man with the iron will, though really he's soft as butter —soft as butter. I *do* like him, too, but I wouldn't trust him with a shilling postal order. Is that all you want to know? I'd like to be off."

"You've been very helpful," said Pibble, lying. "I hope we won't need to bother you again. Can I send for a car to take you back?"

"God, no! And let Mr. Furlough hear about it? I'll take a taxi."

She rose and smiled down on him dismissively, as Catherine the Great must often have smiled at last week's love before sending him off to run and ruin some far province. Go now, the smile said, and I'll retain fond lavendery memories of you; stay and I'll bite. Then she was moving toward the door.

At once Pibble realized why she would never have made an actress; there was something as inherently wrong about her walk as there was about the buttocks of the Etty above his head. He didn't have time to decide where the absurdity lay before she was out the door, and he found he was sighing. He had often marveled at the propensity of a certain sort of staid businessman to run all sorts of social and business risks, to pay out three- and four-figure checks as if they'd been tips to commissionaires, all for the sake of a single night with a certain girl. Who could be worth it? Now he knew.

Wondering whether Ned had come across her, he rang up Sergeant Burnaby and told him about the flat, and about Furlough having it in for Bob Caine, two-minute gobbets that might conceivably be useful. Furlough was said to be very tough indeed. Could he conceivably be moved by the same mad antipathy as affected Pibble?

The afternoon outside the pub was mucky with dust and sticky with a foretaste of rain. The crisp morning, that sense of the world unwrapped from its cellophane, was gone, shredded to tatters with the weary abrasion of workaday minutes. Pibble turned stodgily toward the problems of Flagg Terrace. Assuming Robin's prints were on the bowl, did that mean it must be Robin's shirt? Not necessarily. Memo: ask Eve whether youths have a menial position in the men's hut. Aaron's blood, then? Pibble found he didn't believe it—there was too much, for one thing, and the reaction of the old men had been wrong; they hadn't wanted him to find the bowl, but they hadn't been much worried when he did. It had been something private he'd sleuthed out, something secret, conceivably even shameful. But it hadn't been immediately dangerous to them.

Pibble cheered up slightly when he thought about this. His certainty about the reactions of the black men was encouraging in its tiny way. It was only when you let their differentness hypnotize you that they began to seem impenetrably opaque and strange. He remembered the first interview with the tribe in Eve's bright room, and the waves of psychic force they'd seemed to generate when he made the bloomer about the women, and when he'd tossed the penny; and the way they'd laughed, too—you couldn't call that being secretive about their emotions. And when he'd gone nosing around the men's hut, flooding their shrines with blasphemies of light, the old men's attitude had been subdued, a bit resentful, but tolerant. They had watched him as an elderly gardener might watch his employer poking around in the potting shed. Not Aaron's blood, therefore.

Fernham was at the door of No. 9.

"Glad you're back, sir," he said. "The reports are in from the lab. The fingerprints on the bowl are Robin's, but the blood isn't the old man's—something to do with a hereditary blood disease. And Mr. Thackerey said to tell you the blood-stains made a regular pattern on the back of the shirt, like a herringbone, he said."

"That doesn't sound very nice. I'd better have a word with Robin first, and then I'd like to see the old men one at a time."

"Excuse me, sir," said Fernham, "but I think Dr. Ku would be grateful if you could look in on her for a moment."

"O.K."

As Pibble climbed through the gloom, he heard the noise of furious voices. At first he thought another argument about tribal ritual must be in progress, but at once he realized that the timbre was wrong: this was no deep-lunged Polynesian bellowing, but a mere European yapping. It came from Eve's room. The door was ajar and he went in without knocking.

She was standing with her back to Paul's desk, cornered, beset by the hounds. These were three Englishmen, two of whom were shouting at her when Pibble came in; but they seemed to sense the movement of the big door, for they stopped their clamor in midsentence and stood panting. The one in the middle was an elderly, stoutish figure, wearing a black waistcoat but no collar to his shirt; beyond him stood a younger man in blue overalls, a shortish citizen with a brown face wrinkled like a balloon that has lost most of its air; the nearest man, the one who had not been shouting, was younger still, tidily dressed in a clerkish way, with a pale, sick-looking face and crinkly dark brown hair.

"What's up?" said Pibble.

"Oh, Superintendent," said Eve, "I'm glad you've come. These are three of my tenants who came to inquire about the progress of your investigations and whether the crime is likely to affect the community of Flagg Terrace."

The overalled man marched bouncily across to Pibble. He seemed to be still in the shouting vein, for when he was barely a yard from his objective he gave tongue again.

"You the law rand 'ere, then?"

"I am the officer in charge of this case," said Pibble. "If any of you has any evidence which he believes to be relevant, I shall be interested to hear it."

" 'Ave we *evidence*?" shouted the man in overalls. " 'Ave *we* evidence? An' we bin living amongst 'em these twenny years, some on us. Barnd to come, sooner or later. Yer can't bring a bunch of bleeding savages inner a sillized country and plonk 'em darn an not expeck *sunnick* to 'appen—'s against nature. We bin telling Mrs. Ku 'ere she'll 'ave to clear the lot of em art, an' the sooner the better. I don't care where they goes so long as they goes soon. My missis is scyared to go art of an evening for fear she'll come back one o' these nights with 'er 'ead shrank. They'll 'ave to go or there'll be *real* trouble."

"What is your name, please?" said Pibble.

"Tinker. Jack Tinker. An' this"—he indicated the elderly man with a sidelong sniff—"is Rod Green an' that's Billy Youbegood, as'll bear out what I bin saying, both on 'em."

The elderly man stopped twiddling his front stud and spoke heavily.

"It's not that we're blaming them, mind. They've got a right to murder each other all over the shop, if that's their custom, but they can't come to Flagg Terrace and do it. *And* there's many a day when I smell their cooking and then I can't hardly face me own dinner afterward."

"An' ver *noise*," added Mr. Youbegood. "Clangging and banging till all hours. I got ver top floor in Number eight, next door, an ver racket can be summing heevenish."

"Was there a lot of noise last night?" said Pibble.

"Nah," said Mr. Youbegood. "Night before you should of heard it. Summing chronic, it was, like a beat group run amuck. You hear it, Jack?"

"Can't say I did," said Mr. Tinker. "Tuesday's me night on. But it's typical of the way they goes on, Officer. Unsettling the neighborhood, that's what. Mrs. Ku dint oughter incourage 'em the way she does."

"An' ver la-di-da way vey speaks," chipped in Mr. Youbegood. "Like vat don on ver telly, digging up his bones. What call have vey to go talking like vat?"

"It never has worked," said Mr. Green sententiously, "and it never will work. East is East and West is West, like I keep saying, and the proper thing to do is to keep them apart. Pack them off somewhere else and let them go to the devil their own way."

Pibble's bowels tightened inside him. Ha! The Lord (or, rather, the fluke that a notoriously criminal family in that area had an improbably memorable name) had delivered the enemy into his hand. He went over the top, determined to fight dirty.

"Mr. Youbegood," he said, "how much rent did your wife pay last time you were inside?"

Billy Youbegood gave a small, patient shrug; the defeated gesture of the old lag whom the law will always pick on. But Mr. Tinker reacted into ferocious melodrama, swiveling around on the unembroiled Mr. Green and standing on tiptoe to crow at him.

"I told yer we shouldna brought 'im," he shouted.

"And I told *you*," said Mr. Green with stolid reasonable-ness, "there has to be three of us. Two don't amount to nothing. Well, now, do it, Officer?"

Pibble was glad to have the ball patted so promptly back to him. He had just the right amount of adrenalin spicing his blood, and felt that he could at that moment have abolished the whole Ku Klux Klan down to the last probationary dragon.

"All three of you." he said, "amount to nothing; nothing at all. We'll forget about Youbegood's record and just think of you as three ordinary citizens who've been living for years on the charity of a woman. *You* know, Mr. Green, that there isn't anywhere in London where you could get rooms like you've got for *twice* the money you've been paying. You, too, Mr. Tinker. You just feel you've a right to a soft option. Has either of you ever said thank you to Dr. Ku? I don't believe it. Yet at the very moment she's in trouble, with a close friend murdered in her house, you come round and abuse her because she chooses to help other people, too—other people who have skins of a different color. And I may as well tell you that I am far from convinced that the murder was done by a colored person. It could just as easily have been anyone who had a grudge against colored people—one of you, for instance. So if I hear of you bothering Dr. Ku again, I'll know what to do. I'll put a squad of men on to each of you, with orders to examine every detail about you that they can dig up. They may not turn up a motive for murder, but they'll turn up something, you mark my words. Now clear out, and don't come back unless you've something relevant to tell me."

Pibble opened the door for them, wishing that his fine emotions hadn't come out as a windy sermon backed by an empty threat. Still, Tinker and Green slouched out defeated, and it was left to the despised Billy Youbegood to leave a little more cockily; he'd heard too many lecturings from magistrates to be impressed by a mere Pibble. He grinned at him as he passed and whispered, "Vere's bin somebody out on ver roof evenings."

"Every evening?" said Pibble.

"Nah, but most times when it ain't raining."

"What about last night? And the night before, when there was all the noise?"

"I heard him bofe times—arter ver racket ver first time. Not doing anyfing *our* line—yours an mine, I mean—more like a kid nosing about in summun's yard."

"Thanks," said Pibble. "I'll look into it. How's old Isaac? I suppose he'd be your uncle."

"Passed on, poor old sod. Dropped dead in ver dock wiv shock when ver jury found him not guilty. Receiving, it was, seeing as how he was past anyfing else. So long, ven, be seeing yer."

Pibble shut the door and turned to where Eve leaned against the desk, her arms a black isosceles, looking even more dispirited than when Tinker and Green had been baying at her.

"Where's Paul?" he said.

"In the S.C.R., I imagine. We felt his presence would only make things worse. Thank you for your help. I suppose it was necessary to be so rough with them. Anyway, it can't be mended now; what's done's done. How are you getting on?"

"Slowly. I'd like to ask you a few more questions, if I may. First, do the Kus gamble much?"

"Oh, yes. The men are ready to bet on absolutely anything. The younger ones have taken to horse racing and do quite well, I understand."

"Would the old men bet a few pence on something quite important to them, such as whether I would find a carefully hidden object in their hut?"

"Yes, I think so."

"Next, would a new member of the hut occupy a menial position and have to do things for the old men?"

"Certainly."

"Next, is it true that Aaron wanted you to sell up and move the tribe back to New Guinea, and if so why didn't you tell me?"

Eve straightened and moved away from the desk toward the window. After a couple of steps she bent down, lifted her left heel across her right knee, and fiddled with the strap of her ballet shoe. It was a very elegant pose, asserting all the values of European civilization. It also meant that when she stood and faced Pibble again her face was almost invisible against the afternoon light.

"Yes," she said, "I suppose it was true. But not in the way a fact is true. It wasn't a thing we had ever discussed, except in hints and vague suggestions. My relationship with Aaron was very delicate. We both knew that if we were in agreement the rest of the tribe would do whatever we wanted. But we couldn't afford to disagree, or even to set off along a path that might lead to open disagreement, because then the tribe would disintegrate. I told you that the sense of *belonging* is immensely important to primitive people—to all people, I suspect—but especially to people such as we are; so the tribe, the thing we belong to, has to be preserved intact and Aaron and I had spent all our energies on that one end for over twenty years. We *could* not disagree.

"But, that said, I think it is true that for some time past Aaron had been anxious to return to New Guinea. In fact, I sensed that he had become increasingly anxious about this over recent months."

"Did you have any idea why?" asked Pibble.

"No, except that I think he felt that there was no future for us here as a tribe, and that the best hope was for us all to return to the valley. I feel the opposite, of course; the old men might be able to make the change, but not the young ones or the women, not the children, not I, or Paul."

"Did the problem of what would happen to Bob Caine ever enter into your calculations?"

Eve moved again, over to the window, taking up another ballet dancer's pose against the jamb. It was several seconds before she answered.

"You have a gift for touching tender spots," she said. "There was an episode nearly two years ago when Caine accused Aaron of stealing something from him, but he wouldn't tell me what it was. Aaron behaved like a dignified old lion, but he wouldn't deny the theft. I decided he *had* taken something but didn't regard it as stealing. It was funny, too, because I didn't realize Bob had anything *to* steal. Bob and Aaron had always been very cool toward each other, but they were worse than ever after that, so I have always tended to discount anything they say about each other. But I did have a long discussion with Aaron about six months ago during which he made it clear that he thought Bob was a liability to the tribe, and also that I was somehow maintaining Bob (which, to be honest, I do) in order to appease my father's ghost. He didn't put it like that, of course, or say anything so direct. And I suppose it is true that we feel, all of us, that since Bob precipitated the disaster, the sacrifice must in the end turn out to have been worth while. It's irrational, but strong, strong."

"I see," said Pibble. "Let's move on. You told me Rebecca has a hereditary blood disease: does anyone else have it, or any other like it?"

"Only Robin."

"Who is his father, by the way?"

"Bob. Can't you see the likeness?"

Pibble felt himself go pale. There was gooseflesh on his thighs and calves. Eve must have noticed the change.

"You mustn't blame Bob, Superintendent," she said. "He was very lost and lonely and he came to one of our feasts. He hasn't got a strong head, you know, and they can be very sexually exciting—they are designed to be, in fact. Besides, it has made all the difference to Rebecca's life—not being made love to, I mean, but having a baby, a proper baby, the proper shape with proper fingers and toes. It was the most beautiful thing I ever saw in my life. Please, Superintendent . . ."

Please what? Please understand? No, more than that—please don't muck this bit up, the one tiny piece that's gone dead right for them. Can't be helped. . . .

"Dr. Ku," he said, "I found under the floorboards in the men's hut a bowl of water with a bloody shirt in it. The fingerprints on the bowl are Robin's and from what you tell me the blood must be, too. The pattern of the bloodstains on the shirt is very marked, a sort of herringbone. Does this mean anything to you?"

"Oh God," said Eve. She crossed the room to sit where he had first seen her, on the sofa, and settled into stillness, as still as a stuffed bird in a glass case.

VI

There was something horrible about the priest. Eve was frightened of him from the moment she saw him.

She came out of the school after her first lesson, hot and embarrassed with anger. Daddy had teased her, gently but obviously, in front of all the Kus because of her ignorance of their language and life, and they'd all bayed with happy laughter. Honestly, how could she be expected to know the silly savages would have a special grammar for talking to women with? She was as eager to leave the class, when it was over, as the Kus were to stay. So she came out alone.

He was wringing the neck of a black chicken. He sat cross-legged exactly in the middle of the circle of beaten earth in front of his hut. There was a fire beside him. His elbows stuck out and made rhythmic jerks as he slowly twisted the bird's neck; its wings flapped convulsively, unheeded; he was not looking at what he was doing, but stared with a blind man's stare across the clearing.

The thing that made him horrible was his flesh. It hadn't the black, smooth, slightly oiled roundness of the other Kus, which made her think of slow waves moving under wharves; instead it looked as if it had been puddled together by some-one trying to model in too sloppy clay. His outline was lumpy, irresolute, the lifeless surface obliterating the under-lying curves of muscle and the sharp certainties of bone. Eve assumed he had some beastly disease, like the poor girl who had sat near her in the class.

The school had been built directly opposite the priest's

115

hut, so that his stare seemed fixed on Eve. And because whatever he was doing to the chicken was not the logical way of
killing a bird—the clean half twist and jerk that gets it all
over in a second—Eve was sure that he was performing some
ritual, a malevolent magic aimed at her. She felt that his
uncouth jungly powers had summoned her out of school
at that moment to undergo his attack. She wanted to go back
into school but was ashamed to; she wanted to walk up the
clearing to their own hut, and Mummy, but was afraid to;
so she stood and stared back, feeling sick.

"I wish he wouldn't do that," said Daddy, behind her
shoulder. "Don't be frightened of him, Eve—he's not as bad as
he looks. Come with me and I'll ask him to be kindly dis-
posed toward you. Walk a little behind me and don't stand
on my shadow. He does his little magics with leaves and his
big ones with drums, but he's almost given up the drums now.
He has to do this business with the chicken every new moon,
to renew his powers. We'll wait here till he's finished; it
won't be long now. You mustn't make the mistake of thinking
he's a fraud or a hypocrite—he does know a lot about the
medicinal properties of plants, for one thing—and he lives a
very austere life; there's not many in the Kirk could match it.
But the main thing is he really believes in his powers. And
remember he's had a gruesome training; the wonder is he's
stayed as sane as he has—don't look now."

Eve did look. The priest put the bird's head into his mouth
and bit through the neck. Then he placed the body, wings
still flapping, on the center of the fire; the burning feathers
reeked and crackled. Then he picked up a small pot from
the ground beside him and spat the head into it. Then he
put the lid on. Then he picked up two sticks and with these
lifted another pot from the ashes at the edge of the fire; this
had some sort of wax in it, with which he sealed the lid
down. Then he threw the sticks and a handful of dried

leaves on top of the chicken's body, where they burned with a heavy, herby smell.

Daddy moved forward again and spoke, and the priest replied in the same words; Eve knew two or three of them. The two men began a long ritual of talk.

Close up, Eve saw that the priest was not diseased; instead the whole surface of his skin—face, neck, chest, waist, arms, thighs, shins, and even the backs of his hands and fingers— was covered with a deliberate pattern of scars: old scars made, perhaps when he was almost a child, by shallow sloping cuts which left flaps of skin and flesh loose above them. These had not healed back precisely into place (had not been allowed to, perhaps) and had thus left the surface of the skin alternately puckered and stretched. It must have hurt like mad when it was done, but pity didn't make him seem any less horrible. His eyes, above the wealed cheeks, looked wicked and dangerous. His thin lips barely moved as he spoke. (Ventriloquism was probably one of his "little magics.")

The ticktock talk ended, and Daddy picked his notebook and pencil out of his breast pocket. The priest reached behind him without looking and found a roll of cloth, which he opened; inside were a series of cloth compartments. He held these to his nose and worked along the line, sniffing at each and grunting and chuckling between sniffs. Three times he stopped and took a leaf out. Then he rolled up the cloth, put the three leaves in a row in front of him, scooped a handful of ash from the edge of the fire, and dribbled it in an elaborate pattern around the leaves. As the ash fell, he sang in a shrill, metallic monotone. When the pattern was finished, he picked the leaves from the middle of it, still singing, and erased his work with a stick.

"Come forward now," said Daddy. "Kneel down and cup your hands, where he can reach you."

The priest dropped the three leaves into her hands, making a formal speech about each. Eve didn't understand a word.

"You can stand up now," said Daddy. He was still writing the instructions in his book when Eve turned her back, at last, on the priest.

That night Daddy made her go through the prescribed rigmarole, burning one leaf and smelling the smoke, boiling the other two and drinking the infusions. He explained that the priest might well be able to tell from her behavior whether she had obeyed him, and if he thought she had not she would have a difficult enemy. The burned leaf smelled of resin. One of the infusions was sickly, the other tasteless. Eve slept for fourteen hours and dreamed, as far as she could remember, of nothing at all.

After breakfast she went out to look for the priest and found him sitting in front of his hut again, not doing anything. He was still horrible, still terrifying. The only improvement was that he no longer seemed to be looking straight at her.

VII

Eve came out of her catalepsy almost as soon as she had sunk into it—not more than twenty seconds.

"May I ask you to ask Robin first?" she said. "If he won't tell you, then I will."

"You're keen on who tells, aren't you?" said Pibble. "I suppose that was why it had to be Rebecca who explained about the penny this morning."

"Yes."

"Now, just to save me nipping all over the place, would you tell me if Aaron would have approved of what was going on in the men's hut?"

"Less than anyone."

"He was a very ardent convert?"

"I take it you've seen the picture in his room."

"I think it's very good."

"Paul won't talk about it."

Pibble nodded at the canvases of the heron and the bowler-hatted gent on his right.

"Will he talk about those?" he said.

"Yes. He's excited about them while he's doing them and talks to himself if I'm not there. Afterward he's cynical and tells me exactly how bad they are."

"What about the one he did for me this morning? Would he talk about that?"

"Yes, he's done it several times before—that's why he could do it so fast. It preys on him, you realize, as it does on me; only he can work it off. He got the idea from a Christmas card my nanny sent me, one of the expensive ones, a Brueghel 'Massacre of the Innocents.' She has a genius for the tactless gesture."

"Had the others seen it before?" asked Pibble. "Or Aaron?"

"I don't think so. He always burns them like that; then he talks about them afterward, about the technical difficulties. But he did the picture in Aaron's room in one go, and he has never said a word about it."

Pibble thought about the scattering of smelly and inadequate deities in the men's hut; the contrasting openness and cleanness of the women's hut; the old men retreating down the stairs from Paul's blazing Crucifixion.

"Would Aaron go into the men's hut much?" he asked.

"No, not at all." Eve changed gear into the quick recitative of a scholar rattling through known facts. "In effect, the men's hut is essentially a democratic device, to prevent the chief acquiring too much power. It is analogous, in an elementary way, with a Jacobean Parliament. This is a commonplace among primitive peoples, though it has usually been formalized to such an extent that the people themselves do not recognize its function for what it is; then, in the majority of cases, the appearance of a series of strong chiefs has caused the formality to swallow up the function and the democratic element has ceased to be recognizable as such. Among us, however, largely because the chieftainship is elective (the hereditary system does not root easily in a matrilineal society), the men's hut retains a counterbalancing power against the autocracy of the chief, and this relationship is formalized by a tabu against his entry onto the actual premises. Most of the adult Kus would recognize the basic function of this arrangement without actually formulating it into words, but at the same time they would observe the tabu with a strong sense of awe."

"So Aaron might well not have known what was going on. If anything."

"Oh, he would have known almost at once," said Eve. "And recently he would have heard the drums."

"Billy Youbegood's clanging and banging, you mean. Wouldn't they be doing that anyway? And wouldn't the women have heard?"

"They couldn't use the drums without Robin. There isn't anyone else. The old priest was his mother's brother. And I *have* noticed, now I realize what it means, that the men have been missing during certain television programs which they would normally have watched."

"Who would have started all this off?" said Pibble.

"I cannot think. They're all—well—reasonable, sane, balanced. They are as concerned as I am about the continuance of the tribe as an entity, and they must know this would make it impossible. The women would be outraged. Paul and I . . . Oh, I cannot understand it."

Paul and I what? Outraged, too? Betrayed? Dad betrayed?

"And," said Pibble, "once Aaron was sure this relapse had taken place he would try to do something about it?"

"Certainly. But probably not at once—he liked to mull round problems, for months sometimes."

"It looks as if this whatever-it-is has been going on for months, though; even if it has only just come to a head. Do you think his desire to go back to New Guinea could have anything to do with it?"

"I don't see what."

"Well, do you think the old men would be prepared to kill him if he'd found a way of stopping them from doing whatever it was?"

Eve looked defeated, with all her special knowledge and drearily acquired scholarship in disarray, useless.

"I can't guess," she said. "Yes. If they'd gone as far as to start scarifying Robin, they might do anything. But that really is only a guess, Superintendent. We've been working very slowly in the other direction all these years, and I have

no experience of going back. Poor child. No wonder he preferred not to go to school."

"I'd better talk to him now," said Pibble.

"You'll probably find him in the J.C.R. or the S.C.R.—
downstairs on either side of the front door."

One of the younger women was in the J.C.R., knitting
and watching a small girl who sat in the middle of the floor
and tore a pamphlet from the Citizens' Advice Bureau into
careful strips, which she used to make a nest for a battered
pig from a Noah's ark. Paul was reading *Time* in the S.C.R.
and said Robin had gone down to the basement.

Pibble found him in the men's kitchen, alone. What he
was doing seemed very extraordinary. He sat at the deal
table with a plate of stew in front of him and lapped it up like
a dog; one hand clasped the other wrist behind his back. Surprised by the noise of the door, he looked around over his
shoulder, making no attempt to wipe the congealed stew off
his nose and chin. Pibble went to the stove and felt the stew-
pot; it was not quite cold but distinctly less than blood heat.
Robin returned defiantly to lapping.

"Why are you doing that?" said Pibble.

"It's part of the job," said Robin. "I hear you've found my
shirt, and I suppose you've been to Eve and he's told you what
it's all about."

"Dr. Ku asked me to talk to you first.

"That's right," said Robin, "only I didn't think he would."

"By 'part of the job,' I suppose you mean playing the
drums."

"Sort of."

"Did it hurt a lot when they cut your back?"

"I took four aspirins and they did it with a razor. They
used to do it with a stone knife in the valley, Melchizedek
says."

"Who did it?"

"Ishmael and Daniel. It had to be them because . . . Oh, it's too complicated to explain. Daniel didn't want to, but I talked him into it. But they're all happy about it now. I wowed them with the drums last night, I really did. You know what? I'm the greatest."

"I'd like to hear you."

"Come tonight, man. I'll *wow* you."

"I will if I can. Is it because you're going to play the drums with your hands that you can't use them for eating?"

"That's a bit of it, but really I have to do all sorts of things the wrong way, just to show I'm not an ordinary man like the others. Did you see me make a different sign when I went into the hut this morning? Well, this is like that. It would be easier if I were a monkey and could eat with my toes. Sometimes I think it's not worth it, and I'm not going to go on with it, but that's nonsense."

"How did it start?"

"I wanted to play the drums—like Ringo, you know—and they wanted a priest, so I borrowed a book from Eve to see what it meant. Did you know about Eve? He was dead scared of the drumming man in the valley, before the Japs came, so his dad tried to get him over it by making him study everything my uncle did and putting it in a book. That's what he got his doctorate with. Joke. Well, when I'd read it, I knew that was what I wanted to do—it all seemed so right. I've had to make up a lot, of course; you can't get the right leaves and sticks over here, for one thing. What were they burning in the death lamp this morning? You know, in the wake room?"

"Rubber cable and rosemary were the only things I recognized."

"Not bad. They've got to make a stink, you know, to stop the old man's spirit wanting to come back. You see, it's much harder for me than for the others really to *belong*; I don't look like them, do I? And being priest will make me really belong. They won't be able to do without me."

"You sound as though you belong quite enough already," said Pibble. "Do you really think of Dr. Ku as a man?"

"Of course. It's the way I was taught. There's a fat little dolly in my school called Eve, and I still think it's funny she's got a man's name."

"What are you going to do about eating at school?"

"Oh, that's all right. Outside the house, I'm Robin Ku. It's only inside I'm the priest. It's going to be tricky when I've got to have the scars on my hands and face, but that's a long time yet."

"Is it you who's been getting out on the roof in the evening?"

"How did you know? They're all asleep."

"Billy Youbegood told me. Why aren't you asleep?"

"I don't like beer."

"Will you show me where you get out? It might be important."

"Sure, as soon as I've finished this mess."

Crippen, thought Pibble, what am I going to do about this crazy bit of subplot? N.S.P.C.C., I suppose, though I don't know if they'd take it on. He watched Robin lapping away, quite efficiently. When he'd finished, the boy took two twigs out of his pocket, picked up the plate with them, carried it over to the sink, and ran water over it, tilting it this way and that with the twigs. Satisfied that it was reasonably clean, he lifted it onto a drying rag. Then he went to the hot-water boiler, an elderly coke-burning affair, and threw the twigs into the fire.

"We'll have to get Elijah to let us in," said Robin.

"It shouldn't be locked now."

"Oh. What have you done with the stuff in the bowl?"

"It's gone to the laboratories for analysis."

"I say! That's a nuisance. I suppose it wasn't your fault, but . . . Never mind. I'll think of something."

Fernham was standing at the open door of the hut, bored but used to it. Robin's bed was the pile of blankets in a special little sanctuary over in the farthest corner on the right, beyond the drums. Robin pulled at a piece of painted screening made from an old tea chest, and it slid quietly along the floor; behind it, the wall was only about three feet high under the pitch of the roof, and in the corner was a small door which opened outward into darkness. Robin crawled through; Pibble followed and found himself in a black tunnel; there was a scraping noise ahead, then light; Robin had opened a trap door onto the roof. The tunnel was triangular in section and presumably ran right along that side of the attics between the three-foot inner wall and the actual wall of the house where the roof beams came to floor level. One of these main roof beams, a whopping great thing typical of Flagg, narrowed the triangle of tunnel between Pibble and the trap door, leaving a space he could only just wriggle through.

Outside were the crenelations; they did not look quite so larky close up, being solid and uncrumbled by the sulphurous London air. The stone was granite, not the pitted limestone Pibble would have expected; old Flagg must have imported it specially, probably from Edinburgh at ludicrous expense. Each crenelation was as carefully detailed inside as out. Pibble picked his way along the narrow strip of lead between the sloping slates and the brickwork, peeking out every few steps to get his bearings on the street below, until he was immediately above the porch and (therefore) the stair windows.

He leaned between two slabs of granite and gazed down; with a clack of wings, three pigeons left their perch on a drainpipe four feet below him; beyond that were more pipes—so many that at this angle there seemed to be more metal than brick in places. If Caine had in fact scrabbled his way across the façade, it ought to be possible to see the marks of his passage on the relevant plumbing. It would take, Pibble decided, a whimsically perfectionist mountaineer and murderer to erase his tracks in such circumstances. He craned a bit farther, so that he could distinguish the individual windows, and tried to work out the route Ned Rickard had specified. That must be the vent pipe, which meant that that was the overflow; the latter, to judge by the guano on it, had clearly not endured the tread of man for many years. Elsewhere all the pipes were mottled and splotched in a way which made judgment impossible. An army might have clambered across, each splotch a footprint, or no one at all—you couldn't tell at that distance. Close up, it'd be another matter, but that would mean expensive scaffolding simply in order to justify a police officer's one-sided feud. Pibble withdrew from temptation between the crenelations, like a tortoise retracting his neck.

"Is there another way back in?" he asked.

"There's a trap door over there, in the middle roof, which opens above the stairs, and there's another like the one we got out by round on the far side, but it only takes you back into the hut, and the screen in front of that door's nailed tight. I'll show you when we get back."

Pibble explored the roof. It was an E shape, with the upright backing onto the street and the three arms reaching back toward the garden. Both the other trap doors were bolted on the inside. He jerked himself inelegantly over the party wall and tried the traps of No. 8. The two outer ones were bolted, and the moss on them looked undisturbed. As he was kneeling by the stair trap, it rattled and rose. A pale, sulky head peered at him.

"I wouldn't like *you* to marry my daughter, eiver," said Billy Youbegood.

The trap banged shut. Pibble opened it again and shouted, "Hey!" Billy's head reappeared.

"I only heard noises and fought as I'd better look," he said.

"What are you standing on?"

"Chest o' drors. Full o' junk. Nuffing worf nicking. Don't belong to no one."

"Could anyone else come up there and get out?"

"Not wivout I'd hear vem."

"Billy, there's a lot of lead out here."

"Vere is, ain't vere? Hey! What are you suggesting? Vere ain't none missing, is vere?"

"Not that I can see. But I don't understand how you'd hear a whisper out of their attic in yours, let alone clanging and banging. Not the way these houses are built."

"Ar, for Chrissake," said Billy, "course I been looking round. I got a friend or two in vat line, an' if I got moved out of here it might come in, but I'm not going to be nicking ver roof off my own head, am I? 'Tween you and I, I did take a look round about a monf ago, and vat's when I first heard ver racket vey make—like funder, it was. After vat, I always know when vey're at it. It's not reely a *noise*, but everfing in ver house seems to go shiver, shiver, like ver was an unnerground railway under ver Terrace. Whatter vey up to, d'you know?"

"Playing ritual drums. Thanks, Billy. You're sure no one could have come out through there last night without your hearing?"

"Sure. I got good ears. Uncle Isaac wanted me to be a peterman—combination locks an' such, but I hadn't ver application. Hope you don't mind me asking, but are you Pibble?"

"Yes," said Pibble. "How did you know?"

"Kinky little case like vis. Vey wouldn't send one of ver big boys out on it—too much to lose, nuffing to gain. Good luck, ven."

The head popped back, the trap cracked to, bolts ground home. Yes, kinky and little, just Pibble's line, a typical sidetrack for the excoming man. Ah well, it suited his talents, whatever Mrs. Pibble might say. If he was going to stay and listen to Robin's drumming, he'd have to ring her up soon and make what peace he could. Ah well. Memo: he'd better get Strong to check the exits from the other houses in the Terrace—not that it was important, but somebody might ask. What mattered was the way into No. 9.

He found the tunnel a bit easier to negotiate this time, going under the beam on his back, but realized as he squeezed through that none of the blob-shaped old men could have done it at all. Fernham was out on the landing, tiptoe on a chair to peer at the bolts of the central trap.

"Don't touch it," said Pibble.

"I won't, sir. I just heard you moving about and thought I'd better have a look. There's oldish cobwebs up here, sir. I don't think it's been open for a month or two at least."

"I'll take your word for it," said Pibble. "O.K., Robin. That's all for the moment, thanks."

"Can we have the hut back soon, please?" said Robin. "It'll take ages to get things straight before this evening. Golly, it looks awful like this, doesn't it?"

"Have the lab men finished, Fernham?"

"Yessir."

"Then I suppose that's O.K. by me, Robin. I'd like to come and listen if I may. I suppose it's only fair to say that I shall have to take some sort of action about some of what's been going on."

Robin stopped playing friendly schoolboys. The soft lines of the black visage jump-cut into wary maturity.

"Why?" he said. "What business is it of yours? You get the N.S.P.C.C. to come messing around and you don't get another squeak out of me or any of my old men, I can promise you that."

"You can, can you?"

"Yes."

Um. There seemed to be two Robins: the Ringo fancier, prepared to put up with a lot of pain in submission to the tribal whims of his terrible elders, just in order to be allowed to play the drums; and the jungle drumming man, going through the purgatory of initiation in order to be able to dominate his cackling elders. Or a combination, even . . . Oh, the hell with it. Carry on, policeman.

"So you and the old men have more information you could give me?"

"I expect so. You haven't asked us very much yet."

"Did Aaron know you were doing the drumming?"

"I expect so. He'd have heard the noise, and it had to be me."

"Why?"

"The priest in the village was my mother's brother. I was the only one who *could* do it."

"And it didn't matter who your father was?"

"Not a bit. Haven't you been told we're a matrilineal society?"

Robin produced a long, easy stare, defiant but by no means cocky.

"What else do you know, then?"

"It's not *knowing*—at least not your way, with fingerprints and so on. But it wasn't anyone in the hut, *that's* certain. I was awake all night with my back hurting and I'd've heard them moving."

"Would you? They move too quietly for me."

"They don't for me. I'm one of them."

"What about the women, then?"

"Not a chance. They were all over him, like kids round a teacher, fetching his beer, rolling his fags, running to wipe his nose when he had a cold. They didn't give my old men a look-in. It was dead unfair."

"And Eve and Paul, as you suggested earlier?"

"They'd have to be in it together, wouldn't they? And Eve wouldn't muck up his private zoo for anything. He's got us all in here like rats in a lab, and why should he spoil all that because one old dodderer wants something different?"

"So, according to you, it can't have been anyone in the house?"

"No. There's only one person it could have been, really."

"These aren't facts you've been telling me, you know."

"They'd be facts all right if you'd been living here fourteen years and watching all the little bits and bobs of people's behavior."

And that was true. That was the whole trouble with police work. You come plunging in, a jagged Stone Age knife, to probe the delicate tissues of people's relationships, and of course you destroy far more than you discover. And even what you discover will never be the same as it was before you came; the nubbly scars of your passage will remain. At the very least, you have asked questions that expose to the destroying air fibers that can only exist and fulfill their function in coddling darkness. Cousin Amy, now, mousing about in back passages or trilling with feverish shyness at sherry parties—was she really made all the way through of dust and fluff and unused ends of cotton and rusty needles and unmatching buttons and all the detritus at the bottom of God's sewing basket? Or did He put a machine in there to tick away and keep her will stern and her back straight as she picks out of a vase of brown-at-the-edges dahlias the few blooms that have another day's life in them? Or another machine, one of His chemistry sets, that slowly mixes itself into an apparently uncaused explosion, *poof!*, and there the survivors are sitting covered with plaster dust among the rubble of their lives. It's always been the explosion by the time the police come stamping in with ignorant heels on the last

unbroken bit of Bristol glass; with luck they can trace the
explosion back to harmless little Amy, but as to what set her
off—what were the ingredients of the chemistry set and what
joggled them together—it was like trying to reconstruct a
civilization from three broken pots and a seven-inch lump of
baked clay which might, if you looked at its swellings and
hollows the right way, have been the Great Earth Mother.
What's more, people who've always lived together think that
they are still the same—oh, older of course and a bit more
snappish, but underneath still the same laughing lad of thirty
years gone by. "My Jim couldn't have done *that*," they say.
"I *know* him. Course he's been a bit depressed lately, funny
like, but he sometimes goes that way for a bit and then it
passes off. But setting fire to the lingerie department at the
Army and Navy, Inspector—such a thought wouldn't enter
into my Jim's head. I *know* him." Tears diminishing into
hiccuping snivels as doubt spreads like a coffee stain across the
threadbare warp of decades. A *different* Jim? Different as a
Martian, growing inside the ever-shedding skin? A whole lot
of different Jims, a new one every seven years? "Course not.
I'm the same, aren't I, same as I always was—that holiday we
took hiking in the Peak District in August thirty-eight—the
same *inside*?"

Pibble sighed and shook himself. You couldn't build a
court case out of delicate tissues. Facts were the one foundation.

"O.K.," he said, "I'll try and persuade myself that what's
been happening to you is none of my business if you'll try
and persuade your old men to tell me what they know. I
think I know who your one person is, but it's no use to me
if I can't prove it. I want to talk to Dr. Ku again, and after
that I'd like to talk to the members of the men's hut, one
at a time. They can wait in the S.C.R. until I'm ready for
them; then I'll talk to them in one of the little rooms in the

second floor and pass them up to you to help get things ready. When do you do your drumming?"

"After supper," said Robin. "Could you turn up about half past eight?"

"Fine."

Paul was alone in the bright room downstairs, painting in a curious way, carefully laying thick bars of orange poster paint vertically down a sheet of white paper with a single slow stroke of the brush. They came out marvelously straight and smooth, the paint flowing evenly off the tilted brush as though there were a reservoir in the handle. He worked across the sheet until all its white innocence was behind bars; then he put his brush down, turned the paper around through a hundred and eighty degrees, and studied each bar in turn. At last he crumpled the sheet up and threw it on the floor; there were about twenty balls of colored paper already there.

"What are you up to?" said Pibble.

"Learning. Practicing as a child practices the violin. I began late and I have much to learn. Eve has gone for a walk. He is upset."

"I'm sorry."

"The time was coming, even if Aaron had not died."

"You mean the tribe would have decided to break away from her—him and gone back to New Guinea anyway."

"Perhaps."

"Which side were you on?"

"Side?"

"Do you think they should go?"

"I do not want them to go. They are necessary to my work. I flower out of their decay, out of *our* decay. Furthermore, I want what Eve wants; we are a very harmonious couple, Superintendent."

Silence, though the afternoon air seemed filled with the

impregnation of his soft, prodigious bass, as though the salts of it were suspended in a solution of stillness.

"You didn't answer my question," said Pibble.

"Your question had no meaning, which was why I answered with an account of my own selfishness. The tribe cannot be considered as a living entity, Superintendent, susceptible to words like 'should' and 'ought.' It is not dead yet, but it is in a state of coma from which it will never awake. The people here, insofar as they are people, are worth thought and trouble. But to a great extent they do not consider them-selves as people but as organs of a larger body, a body which was smashed in an accident twenty-five years ago and breathes still only through the combined miracle of Aaron's will and Eve's skill. This house is an iron lung."

"They have started some sort of drumming ritual in the men's hut," said Pibble.

"How? Oh, of course, with Robin using the drums. Did Aaron know?"

"Eve and Robin think so. Didn't she—he tell you?"

"Use the feminine, Superintendent. Aaron would not have liked the sound of the drums. It was a sign of the will begin-ning to lose its hold on the flesh. I told you the time was coming."

"What could he have done to stop it?"

"He could have . . ."

Silence again. Paul chose a fresh brush, a tiny one, and dabbled it carefully in a jar of floor stain. Then with a quick swoop he drew one huge "O" on the clean sheet before him. The brush went back into its holder, and he picked up a two-foot rule and measured his circle this way and that.

"Do you admire Giotto, Superintendent?" he said.

"I like his paintings very much."

"I, too. But, as you imply by your half answer, the story

is unworthy of him. It is too easy to draw what looks like a circle, too difficult to draw what is one."

"Aaron, Paul."

"I was wrong, Superintendent. He could *not* have held a meeting of the whole tribe and used his weight as chief to forbid the drumming, because that weight was part of the world to which the drumming belongs. His authority as chief grew out of the same roots as the priest's powers as drummer; if Aaron had a right to forbid the drumming, then Robin had a right to drum. He could have argued, but I cannot see what arguments he could have used. Even the Reverend Mackenzie did not forbid the drumming—he just enticed us away, and when the priest found us coming no more, he laid his drums aside."

"Enticed you?"

"There may be a better word, Superintendent. It is difficult to explain. The Reverend Mackenzie was, to a simple people, a magician. I now realize that much of his magic was hypnotism, but I do not think he knew this himself. We had had a missionary before him, the Reverend Smith, a good man; I was his houseboy; he worked hard and he died. We believed our priest had killed him with the drums, but did not much care. Then the Reverend Mackenzie came. The chief—his name was Akotapolulo—arranged that we should greet him formally, with the whole people there. He walked between us, spoke to the chief in the dialect of a tribe down the valley—quite like our own language—and to the priest. Then he knelt and prayed aloud in his own language, among us all, and then he stood up and looked along the men's side. His eyes found me and he called me to show him his hut. I was dressed no differently from the other boys—our tribe wears no clothes—but he picked me out, the houseboy of the old missionary, and I led him to his hut. Within two days, any of our people who were in the village would be watching all the time out of the edge of their eyes in the hope of seeing the Reverend Mackenzie moving between his hut and the school, or the school and the altar he was building under the big tree. He made it all with his own hands and would not let us help. Soon it was as if we had a god living among us. The hunters tried to touch him before they went out onto the mountain, and women before childbirth would beg me to steal some belonging of his for them to hold during their pains. And all of us tried to earn his pleasure by doing what we believed he wished, though he seldom made his wishes directly known to us. In the end the priest, too, put his drums away and worked only with leaves and the fire. He was trying to use the drums again when the Japanese shot him. I found him in the middle of them."

"Are the drums wicked?"

"They are *different*, Superintendent. As different from Christianity as my skin is from yours."

"Why didn't the whole tribe hide?"

Paul took a razor blade and scratched out a tiny line where an errant hair from the brush had spoilt the round of his "O."

"I do not know for certain," he said. "Akotapolulo was dead, and it was decided between Moses and the men's hut and the Reverend Mackenzie. But the place where a tribe lives is a holy place, twice holy, since the Reverend Mackenzie also lived there. One does not readily desert it, any more than monks left their shrines when the Goths came. I think they decided that the danger was not great, that the Japanese would probably not come at all. But Bob had to hide, and enough of our people had to go with him to tend him, so it seemed wise to make the party a fairly large one, but not large enough for it to be obvious that people were missing. Then, provided every trace of Bob's presence was removed, all should be safe. When I went to the village after the Japanese had gone, I found the Reverend Mackenzie hanging from his own doorpost, with a packet of Bob's cigarettes stuffed between his teeth. I have never told Eve."

Pibble refused to think about it. "You mentioned Christianity," he said. "I gather that Aaron was a very ardent Christian. Why would he want to take the tribe back to New Guinea?"

"Because he had heard the drumming, I think. He may have felt that Christianity had failed to flourish here as it did in the valley, and that we must therefore go back and start again where the Reverend Mackenzie stopped, and make a Christian tribe growing on its own roots in its own soil. He may have felt, as I should if I did not have Eve and my work, that nothing that happened here was real, that most of us would die and the rest would be assimilated, and the tribe would be lost like beer spilled on gravel, and with the tribe the Reverend Mackenzie's work would be lost, and then all would be as if the Reverend Mackenzie himself had never come and lived among us and changed our lives. We are an anthropological mutation, Superintendent. The Reverend Mackenzie was a cosmic ray which strikes by chance upon the genetic apparatus of some plant—perhaps a small, dull yellow flower which hitherto has flowered only with a single row of petals—and makes it flower double. Then came the frost, and Eve transplanted us to this greenhouse, where we pine. So Aaron wanted to move us back into our own soil, now that the frosts are gone. Possibly his motives were something like that. You distrust analogies?"

"Usually."

"I, too. But the Reverend Mackenzie was a phenomenon of that order. Look."

Paul leaned sideways and took a fat folder of papers from a bottom drawer. They were artist's studies, the top ones mostly of cats. Below the felines came the people: a brilliant but affectionate caricature of Billy Youbegood; several Kus, done in techniques ranging from many-lined scratchings to five strokes of a brush; lots of studies of Eve; one drawing of a bearded man in a floppy hat.

"I used a photograph, of course," said Paul.

Pibble was disappointed. Thin face, eyes rather close, high cheekbones, the body-jointing oddly ungainly—you could read anything into the picture, anything you already believed to be there. He stared at the sketchy lines suggesting a crumpled tropical jacket and willed some clue to emerge, some certainty, either the dynamic saint witnessed by Paul and Caine or the selfish don he had sensed lurking between the lines of Eve's absurd fragments of biography. He found nothing, and handed the sheet back to Paul.

"A hypnotist, you think?" he said. "That might account for the way you all speak English. Hypnosis would help, wouldn't it?"

"It did," said Paul. "But we all lapsed badly as soon as the Reverend Mackenzie died. I think we would have forgotten the language entirely, or reverted to some form of pidgin English, but for Aaron. He was a very dedicated man and drove us back into the grammar of righteousness. Nothing that the Reverend Mackenzie had achieved must be lost, he felt."

"But he seems to have gone through remarkable contortions to keep the vision alive," said Pibble. "Like St. Paul, I suppose. Will you tell Dr. Ku that I was looking for her? It isn't urgent. This thing will take a day or two yet."

Paul grunted—a deep, wild noise like a lion's hiccup—and started to lay a flat wash of green across his "O," stopping with a gymnast's precision at the exact edges. Pibble watched, half bemused, half simply idling, happy to watch anything provided that it was in no way related to Aaron's murder. He was suddenly sure that the whole business was going to end in misery. The knowledge shook him into leaving.

As he went down the dusky stairway, he realized what was wrong with his case: he didn't want to catch anybody if it wasn't going to be Caine, and he didn't believe it was—though Robin seemed to think so. Always a bit deficient in the hunting instinct—more of a herbivore than a carnivore, as detectives go—this time he simply didn't care whether anyone was arrested or not. Interesting setup, of course; curious people. That was part of the trouble; it was only a sort of scholarly inquisitiveness that kept him asking questions and nosing about; the purpose behind the questions seemed increasingly irrelevant, the murder hunt a distraction from the real thing. Dammit, he was much more interested in the prospect of watching the drumming ritual than he was in questioning the old men.

That being so, he decided, who would he like to talk to next? Somebody normal, for God's sake, who'd give him tea and not badger his sensibilities with prehistoric woes. Mrs. Caine seemed the only candidate.

Outside the westering sun was off the street, and the shadows of the crenelations above him marched evenly across the surface of the opposite façade, repeating the pattern of solid stone above them like a visual echo in an early Dali. He was just starting down the steps toward Cora Lynn when he realized that it would be kinder and more convincing if he rang Mrs. Pibble up now. The unvandalized booth was empty this time.

"Hello, darling. Sorry to disturb you. Look, I'm afraid I'm going to be late home tonight, if you can stand it. . . . No, nothing like that. . . . I'm sorry; can't you put it in the fridge? . . . I'll tell you when I see you; it's a very odd business, and if I keep going I might . . . Yes, of course. . . . I'm sorry. . . . Is there anything you want me to do? . . . I'll write to her tomorrow. . . . No, it's very interesting, but not the sort of thing that makes the newspapers. Except the

West Kensington *Gazette,* I suppose. . . . Ah well, life's like
that. How're things with you?. . . O.K., I'll tick him off
at the weekend. . . . How can I? There isn't going to be
a moment when we're both about before then. . . . I'm
sorry. . . . About eleven, I should think. Don't keep your
light on. . . . Bye, then. I love you. . . . Bye."

Minute by minute they live, and every minute a brick
which they carefully fit together into a wailing wall.

The door of the basement flat was open. Mrs. Caine sat
at the kitchen table, her spectacles clinging absurdly to the tip
of her inadequate nose as she stitched at a pair of crimson
pajamas. There was something clumsy about the way she was
doing it. Ah, yes, the plaster on her thumb made it difficult
for her to hold the needle. She looked up with the same sharp,
suspicious twist of the head she'd used that morning, then
smiled and put her work down.

"Good afternoon, Superintendent. Did Bob find you? He
hasn't come back."

"Yes, he did. I expect you're too young to know the tradition that a policeman visiting a kitchen expects a cup of tea."

"A cup of tea from the cook and a kiss from the housemaid. We have no cook or housemaid, I'm afraid, but I'll
put a kettle on for you. Are you sure you don't want
whisky?"

"Tea's what I want, if it's not a nuisance."

"Course not. Bob drinks quarts of the stuff. I'll have some
Nescafé. Sit in the armchair and I shan't fall over you."

Small chance of that, thought Pibble, watching her do her
cooking trick; she hardly moved a step to get kettle and milk
onto the gas, then mugs, spoons, tea, Nescafé, milk, sugar,
teapot, and biscuits onto the table. Accustomed to Mrs.
Pibble's flurried dashes to unrelated cupboards, he found the
process fascinating. Often she did not have to look before
reaching the right container off a shelf.

"Do you run your whole life like that?" he said.

"Like what?"

"A place for everything and everything in its place, and all in easy reach."

"Oh, does it look like that?"

She laughed—a curious noise, more like the preening coo of a pigeon on a June morning than anything else, made with her small mouth opened to an "O" and the tips of her tiny teeth just showing and looking as sharp as a puppy's.

"I was just talking," said Pibble.

"Honestly," she said, "I'm not one of those people who think about themselves very much. I don't mean I'm not selfish, but if I want something I want it and don't wonder why. Sometimes I read an article somewhere about psychology—one of the TV critics in the Sundays goes on and on about it—and I don't say, like my pa does, what a load of drivel. I just think, Goodness, all that's going on inside me without me having the slightest idea. Like digestion, sort of, and I don't think about my kidneys very much, either. I suppose the answer to your question is yes, in a sort of way. I don't like to find things sensibly arranged, but I like to leave them like that. Give me a good old-fashioned attic, where people have been putting things for twenty years to get them out of the way, old wickerwork cots and dressing-up clothes and iron bedsteads and horrible green glass vases and trunks full of albums and diaries and other trunks full of tropical uniforms and marble washstands and picture frames and nursery fireguards and broken deck chairs and wooden-shafted golf clubs, and so on, and I'll be happy for a week. I like a jungle to tidy, but once it's tidy I like to move on. I suppose that's why I picked Bob. He'll *never* be in the same place I put him down; he's even more of a mover-on than I am. Foundations of a stable marriage, believe it or not. How many spoons shall I put in?"

"A couple would be fine."

Again the cooing laugh. "Bob likes six," she said. "How are you getting on next door?"

"Difficult to say," said Pibble. "Thanks, that's super. It's a jungle all right, but I don't much feel like tidying it; I'd much rather just watch it. Do you know Robin at all?"

The effect was like hail at a garden fête, prattle and parasols one moment and a scurry for shelter the next. Mrs. Caine's small features, animated so far like those of a little girl in her granny's feather hat, became pinched and suspicious.

"You know Bob's his father?" she said.

"I'm sorry," said Pibble. "I didn't mean anything police-like by bringing him up. It was just an example of the fascination of the jungle. Here's this schoolboy who's managed to set himself up as a sort of spiritual adviser to a group of great-uncles because his mother's brother had been the village priest before they were converted to Christianity. One moment he's eagerly showing me round the roof, and the next he's threatening me with complete withdrawal of assistance by himself and his flock."

"How could they help?"

"Oh, by telling me things. The old men treat it as a sort of game and bet with each other about how much I'll find out. Robin, at least the priest Robin, takes it more seriously. He says he could name the murderer, if he chose."

"Could he?"

"I think so. I don't think he could actually prove it yet, but I think he and his old men know enough between them to make a reasonable case, once you'd added on all the police nonsense about fingerprints and such."

"And without his help you haven't a clue?"

"I've got lots of clues, but none of them adds up to anything. I need the sort of push that will make me pick up the ones which matter. You know, like a good photograph of an

apparently boring building, which tells you what the architect thought he was up to. If you look at it from here, in
this kind of light . . . Robin could very well give me that
sort of angle on the whole business. Eve ought to be able
to, but she's so determined not to prejudice me in any direction that she only adds to the confusion."

"Wouldn't one of the old men do as well?"

"Unlikely. I'm going to talk to them all, one at a time,
after tea, and I bet you when I'm finished I'll be no further
on than I am now. They don't take it seriously, and I never
have the slightest idea if they're telling the truth."

"When d'you think Robin will come up with the goods?"

"Your slang is curiously out of date for one so young. I
bet your father reads Wodehouse aloud."

"Bang on, Hawkshaw. He does all the different voices,
too, quite beautifully. You should hear him as Gussie Fink-
Nottle giving away the prizes. It drives poor Bob round the
bend; he can't stand it; he always slopes off to the pub at
reading time. Will Robin blow the gaff soon?"

"I don't know. Maybe tonight. He's a bit preoccupied
with his drumming this evening; then he usually goes out
on the roof to cool off."

"Drumming?"

"Part of his job as priest. They do it in Haiti—for Voodoo
purposes, I've read—and this seems to be the same sort of
thing. All the men think it's very important. I'm going to
listen to it this evening, with luck."

"What does Eve think about it?"

"She seemed very shocked when I told her, and Paul says
she's upset, though she's got a right to be that anyway."

"Didn't she know about it before? She must have heard it."

"You know what these houses are like. Billy Youbegood,
on your top floor, says he first heard it when he was out on
the roof looking for lead to nick, and now he can tell if it's

going on by the vibration, but I don't think Eve knew about it. She's two floors down, and the women spend most evenings watching the telly. As an anthropologist, she ought to be all agog about it, but I think she'd like to stop it; only she can't do anything until they've chosen a new chief—that's to say she thinks she can't, though I'd have thought she had the whip hand if it came to an argument."

"Bob always says she's utterly helpless without a man around."

And that was true. He'd used almost those words. Pibble, so expansive a moment ago, shrank into himself like a disturbed anemone, one of those blobs of unresponsive jelly which disappointed children poke at in rock pools. The sensation was so sudden and so fierce that he was sure a physical spasm must have rippled across his features, plain for Mrs. Caine to see if she hadn't been at the stove refilling his teapot.

"Doesn't Paul count as a man?" he said.

"I don't know. Bob hates Paul; isn't it funny? He hates him worse than Aaron, and he always used to say Aaron was a thief. He's got a bee in his bonnet about them both."

"What did Aaron steal?"

"A . . . Oh, I don't really think he stole anything. He was such an honorable old boy. But Bob lost a lucky mascot which he'd had all through the war, and he convinced himself that Aaron took it."

"And what about Paul?"

"I'm not at all sure about that, either, but Bob's always had a roving eye, you know, and there they were alone in the jungle, two white people among a lot of savages, and in a film they'd have finished up falling into each other's arms; only in real life Eve preferred Paul. Lucky for me, but bad luck on Bob. She's rather special, don't you think? And she still will be when I'm a fat old crone. Is that you, darling?"

Pibble heard a cough and a shuffling in the hall, rather stagy, a noise made by someone who meant to be heard. Eve put her head around the door.

"May I come in, Susan?" she said. "I think the Superintendent wants to talk to me."

"Super," said Mrs. Caine. "You're just the excuse I need to make the Superintendent a fresh pot of tea. Do you ever get on Christian-name terms with people before you arrest them, Superintendent?"

"Not yet," said Pibble. (And not this time, please God.) "I'm sorry to bother you, Dr. Ku, but there are two things I really need your help on. The first one hasn't got anything to do with the murder directly, but I've landed myself in a spot over Robin. I ought to tell the N.S.P.C.C. people what's been going on, but he's rather cornered me into not doing so. Still, I must do something or I shan't sleep easy, but I don't know what. Have you got any ideas?"

Eve sighed and settled into one of her ballet poses on the tall kitchen stool.

"I have been brooding on that also," she said. "Do you know if the men forced him into being priest?"

"I don't think so," said Pibble. "If anything, he maneuvered them into having him, but mostly it was something that suited them all."

Eve sighed again. "That makes the moral issue no clearer," she said. "Left to myself, I think I would do nothing; any action must cause a greater upheaval, a worse derangement of the pattern. But I see you must do something. You had best tell Rebecca what has been happening, and leave her to act. I think she will do whatever it is that turns out to be for the best, and she's the only person Robin will take interference from. The priest is very much set apart from the rest of the tribe, but as he cannot marry he tends to develop a forceful relationship with his mother; many of his powers are felt to stem through her. I don't know how much Robin knows. . . ."

"He got most of it out of a book you wrote," said Pibble.

"Ah, yes, I see—my doctorate thesis. I did lend him that. What pits one digs for one's own feet. When I wrote it, I thought how pleasant to think that it was all now history, dead and buried. How could I have foreseen this loathsome ghost walking? How could I?"

"Here's your tea, Eve," said Mrs. Caine. "You mustn't think that she's specially favored, Superintendent, having a cup when you've only got a mug, but she doesn't have milk or sugar, so I keep our only cup for her, and even that doesn't have a saucer."

"What is it?" said Pibble, glad of a little chitchat to give Eve a chance to recover from her agonies. The cup was the thinnest imaginable china with a green and violet parrot on it. "Meissen? It's very pretty."

"Not bad, Hawkshaw. Nymphenburg, actually. I got it in the Portobello."

"If Robin's read my book with care," said Eve, "he will be very impressed by his mother's wishes. I don't know how much he actually *believes*, and how much is just make-believe, but theoretically Rebecca could withhold a lot of his powers from him. They are transmitted through her, you see; the hereditary ones, that is. I wonder how they managed the earliest steps of initiation. I can't ask myself, but if he tells you I should be most interested to know."

Her voice was dry and controlled. The scholar, when cholera ravishes his children, retreats to the dust of the library.

"Well, I'll talk to Rebecca, then," said Pibble. "The other thing I wanted to consult you about is more complicated. It seems to me probable that whatever motive there was for murdering Aaron was connected with the revival of this drumming ritual. Everyone who knew him agrees that he would have wanted to stop it, and I think it's possible that one of the steps he would have taken to try and stop it might have been so inconvenient to somebody that they decided to kill him. It also seems that he was thinking, and had been for some time, of trying to persuade you to move the tribe back to New Guinea, and that this was somehow bound in with the process of stopping the drumming. Does any of this make sense to you?"

"I've been talking to Paul," said Eve. "I only just missed you when you left. You will have discovered by now that we are all—to some degree, at any rate—obsessed with my father. I had not realized how much the others were before; it is, of course, natural for me. Aaron, Paul thinks, was more obsessed than any of us. He was a difficult man to explain to a European, though not an uncommon type among peoples with a pre-urban mode of thought. He was both intelligent and simple. If I said that he held his beliefs with the intensity of a peasant, I would be putting a wrong image into your mind, but you must think of something of that order; think of those dingy, relic-crammed chapels in the parched south, where the hills are steep and barren and the richer soil in the narrow valleys is owned by hundreds of cousins in hundreds of tiny parcels. The peasants there have something of Aaron's kind of faith, believing with passion in the virtues of their own chapel's precious fragment of the veil of Saint Chrysostoma. But Aaron's relic was my father; he had talked with him, learned from him, knew his virtues as real in the real world, and not just erratic emanations from a capricious heaven. We think, Paul and I, that he must have felt that the soil of the valley where my father had walked had a special virtue; that that was where Daddy had chosen to do his life's work, and that it had been a sort of sacrilege to abandon the shrine (though, in fact, we did so at Aaron's bidding). If I am right, he would have applied his considerable intelligence to possible means of moving the tribe back. He would have looked for a little advantage here and another little advantage there. It was at his wish that we originally got an estate agent to have the Terrace valued, for instance."

"What would the obstacles have been?" asked Pibble. "I imagine Paul's work would have been a major one."

"Curiously, no," said Eve. "Or at least I don't think so. I don't think he ever realized the quality of Paul's work. The picture of the Crucifixion was just a picture of a holy subject to him; a cheap print might have met his needs just as well. Paul's picture has a particularly startling meaning to us, of course, but Aaron would have been satisfied with a much cruder drawing which bore the same interpretation. The position of the artist in a primitive community is a very different thing from his position in a civilized city, Superintendent. In some ways, the village artist is much happier; art, to us, is an ordinary part of the ritual of living, and the man who is painting a picture, or practicing a gymnastic dance, is in our eyes doing an ordinary job of work, just as much as the man who is snaring lizards or thatching a hut; his place in the community is accepted, normal, and he can just get on with his job. This is a much healthier state of affairs than prevails in Western civilization. On the other hand, the position of the artist who happens to be an outstanding practitioner is much less fortunate; innovation is difficult and constricted in the framework of a ritual tradition; the opportunities for cross-fertilization between cultures are rare; the audience is receptive and uncritical, quick to appreciate nuances inside the tradition but baffled by anything outside it. I believe that Paul is an exceptional artist, but I do not think Aaron had even thought about the idea. He was amused that Londoners should pay so highly for our tribal art, but he would have expected Paul to be just as happy and fulfilled back in the valley decorating the doors of huts."

"I see," said Pibble. "Then what other boulders would he have tried to shift?"

Eve glanced sideways toward where Mrs. Caine was sitting, not seeming to listen at all, nibbling at a bitten-to-the-quick little-finger nail.

"There was that other thing I talked to you about in our house. Aaron was certainly obsessed with the idea that I gave greater attention to the matter than I should. I think he might well have decided to try and find a method of convincing me that the relationship involved was deleterious. I have been thinking, while I was out walking, about your conjuring trick this morning which so impressed us all, and it does seem to me possible that Aaron was going to try and use his evidence (if evidence it was) to detach me from that particular reason for staying. It would have been pointless, but he could not have known that."

Just like doing an easy crossword puzzle. The relationship was with Caine, the evidence was the penny, the conjuring trick was tossing it. What the hell did Mrs. Caine make of it all, if she was listening?

"Because he couldn't understand about Paul?" he said.

"When we were still on the island," said Eve, "he came to tell me one day about his plans for the future of the tribe, because they affected me. He was always secretive, but very honorable, too; he would not have thought it right to involve me in one of his schemes without my knowledge. Then I discovered that he had really no conception of the nature of my relationship with Paul. . . ."

VIII

I am an addict, thought Eve. I am addicted to Paul. So young, so young, so young, under the razzle-dazzle leaves. I'll take us all to London and buy a proper bed, a brass one with knobs you can unscrew and leave messages in. The inside of the rims of his eyelids are red; as red as . . . as . . . as a rose. Paul scarlet. My love is like a black, black rose. You can shut your eyes and feel the color of his skin, through your fingertips and the palms of your hands, black as . . . as . . . Oh hell! Like suède, sort of; but not, sort of . . . velvety. It's the extra cutaneous layers they have because of the sun. Bet you white men feel like the inside of sponge bags; can't imagine being addicted to the inside of a sponge bag. Never know now. Have to deduce all men from Paul, being all things to all men, all men to all things. Daddy said you mustn't argue about God as if there were more than one. I believe in one God, to Whom statistics therefore do not apply. Thus, therefore, it follows . . . it follows . . . it follows . . . it—only one Paul in my universe, no other portent in my small sky. Or is it only a pash? Could it be for anyone, for Humphrey Bogart or a history mistress or the Duke of Windsor? His breath smells of cinnamon. Oh Christ, what can I do with them all? Why should it have to be me? I want to go away and live alone with Paul, alone in a civilized country where you can buy brass bedsteads. And what do you propose to do to earn your bread, Miss Mackenzie? Man cannot live by bed alone, still less two men. And Bob, please God, will go back to Australia and we'll never hear or see or think about him again, except to send him a telegram when he gets his D.S.O. Poor Bob.

Six months now—a pash couldn't last six months, surely. If you're under a strain and all your friends are being killed and there isn't enough to eat, then you might fall into the nearest man's arms just because he was handy, but we stuck all that time out. And we stuck out three feasts, too—not like feasts in the village, but even so—hope Mummy and Daddy enjoyed themselves after the feasts in the village; I wonder what Mummy made of it all. Four feasts, if you count the first moon feast we weren't allowed to go to, and they didn't even turn a hair because they were so pleased to have a couple of sentries; wonder if Aaron had thought of that, too, the wily old ape. They've got subtle minds, only they don't use them the same way. Sometimes I know what he's thinking now; I know when he's happy. Funny, three nights of drink and shouting and dancing and we didn't even hold hands, and then we stumbled against each other on the path up to the lizard traps and both said yes together. Soggy, that's what I am, soggy with love. If I take him—them all—to London, he'll have to have something to do which he's happy doing, not for money but just for his mind to grind on; otherwise it'll grow round and round into itself like a rabbit's teeth and bury itself in his own skull. What can you do with patterns? Fabrics and wallpapers and things, I suppose —there must be technical schools which teach people. And I'll write a book about Daddy, except that I don't know enough about it all, but they must teach that, too; they must teach everything. Now we move on in our next lecture to a curious and rather repellent aspect of the Thames Valley Culture, the ritual segregation of females of the higher castes at puberty into establishments known as Colleges, where they lived for five years and worshiped the minor deity called Pash. He knows what I'm thinking, too. He's a saint. His skin tastes bitter, like burned herbs. If we could go away and live together, we could have children and not be ruled by this miserable rhythm. It's always been the men poets who made such a fuss about the moon. I must ask Aaron whether a hunting Ku has ever had a baby—there might be something in the myths, and then life would be simpler. He's ambitious, that's the word, not like the other Kus; he wants to do whatever he does as well as it can be done, not just as well as it's always been done. There's no scope for him here, in this tiny crumb of a tribe. Edinburgh. If there's enough money. How rich *was* Mummy? I wonder if he'll get fat when he's old, as fat as the old men. It depends how I feed him, or perhaps it's hereditary—I must keep notes. And in London we'll be able to feed Becca properly, though it's too late, surely. He walks like a clever toy. It's the way they put their feet down which makes them move so quietly. I'll get him to draw me pictures of a Ku walking and pictures of Bob walking and see if he can see the difference. Lucky Bob gets incapable so early at the feasts—wonder if he's worked it out yet about me and Paul; bet he has. Bob's not really stupid— that's the wrong word—hell to teach, a scowling lump at the back of the class, but cunning about people—bet Bob knew before Aaron, if Aaron knows now. Funny, Aaron's *clever* —scholarship class, given the chance—but simple about people; he can count their leaves and their sepals but he cannot feel how their roots writhe between the crumbs of soil. Paul can. If I tried to write him down, it'd come out all wrong, a noble savage, a tender orangutan, a super collection of scooped muscles and tingling skin, a love animal—all wrong. I never looked at Bob properly till Paul drew him in the dust. Poor Bob.

If Paul agrees about going to Edinburgh, or even London, we'll have to talk to Aaron. It really would be for everyone's good, it really would; get away from all this and forget about the miseries and find a nice, big house in the Wynds where we can start all over again. When Paul gets back from the coast—please, God, keep him out of trouble. Please. Please—they killed Pastor Bollern, too, and all his people; we weren't the only ones. Five days to the river, say, and three days on makes eight and two to find out and eight back—why doesn't it ever come out different?—eighteen. Eleven, he's been gone, eleven, eleven . . . Buck up, Mackenzie! When Paul—

"Miss Mackenzie."

She rolled onto her back and sat up. Aaron stood black and squat amid the bower of creepers which they had found not far from the trail to the lizard traps.

"Is Paul back?" she said.

"Soon, perhaps. He need not go all the way to the coast, I think. Elijah found one of the Amalotoluto fishing down in our marshes, who said that the Japanese are gone."

"Gone?"

"Gone from all the island. If this be true, Miss Mackenzie, what must we do next?"

"Oh Lord, Aaron, I don't know. I'll have to go to England, I suppose, and find out what's happened to everything, and I'd like Paul to come, too."

"We must all come. We must go far from here and learn to be a new people in a Christian land."

"But what'll you all *do*? The men can't go out hunting all day—there's nothing except fields and houses. If you found a new valley here—"

"A new valley here would be as the old valley, Miss Mackenzie. We are too few and the Reverend Mackenzie is dead. Soon we would be lost, dried up as a puddle is dried by the sun. We must go to a different place, where we have nothing but ourselves. There our loneliness will hold us together. Paul must join the men's hut once more and wed with Rebecca, and you must wed a man of your own people."

"Sikataro kani takarato Paul ni plarai pikaru ni kala tai!"

Aaron grunted and stared at her, clawing deeply at the side of his beard. When they got to Edinburgh, Paul would have to start shaving; that'd help to set the two of them really apart from the rest. Aaron grunted again and wheeled away, like a pachyderm confronted by a motorcar. Eve realized what had happened; he had thought his campaign out in detail, right down to the subjunctives in the sentences, and now the whole scheme had come to pieces over a minor tactical defeat. He'd go away and piece together another scheme which allowed for her aberrations. She wondered what his mental picture of England was like—Mummy had often talked to him about it, making extra coaching in English an excuse for dreamy nostalgia—and anyway the war would've made everything quite, quite different. She rolled over onto her stomach again, but could not recover the dozy, sensual wash, half thought, half dreamed, which had kept her happy before Aaron came. Instead she watched two ugly, clumsy beetles, impeded by their own ill-fitting wing sheaths, blundering through the process of mating as though nobody had ever thought of it before.

IX

"I'm sorry. Where was I? Oh, yes—in the same way I think he had no conception of Paul's relation with his work. He would have considered it perfectly natural for him to return to New Guinea and use his talent decorating the doors of a few huts."

"Didn't he talk to you about any of this, Mrs. Caine?" said Pibble.

She abandoned her tortured nail, like an old lady laying her crochet work down in her lap to cope with the importunities of a great-nephew.

"Aaron?" she said, with a curious squeaky giggle that he hadn't heard before; it seemed strangely out of context. "He was always talking about going back to New Guinea, but I never thought it was more than a daydream."

"He didn't talk about it any differently last night?"

"Not that I noticed, but honestly I'd slightly given up listening. I enjoyed having him here, but I'd heard it all before, about the pig hunts and the hut building and the dances and feasts and drums—"

"Drums!" said Eve sharply.

"Yes, and having the whole valley full of jungle round them and it all being theirs for miles and miles and miles. He used to talk about the children growing up with that as the world they knew, instead of all these bricks."

"But he didn't say anything new last night?" said Pibble.

"I didn't *hear* anything. It was like having a record player

154

on playing Beethoven, but you don't pay any attention to
it because you're doing a crossword or worrying about money
or something. It's not right, and you know it, just treating
all that marvelous stuff as a cozy noise, but you do it because
you feel like it."

She laughed her proper pigeon laugh this time.

"Are you sure that he talked about drums as if they were
something he liked?" said Eve.

"Yes, I think so. No. Wait a bit—it's all my fault for not
listening properly—he might have said that somebody else
had them and he didn't like them. Was there another tribe
anywhere near? Anyway, I don't think he talked about them
at all last night."

"Never mind," said Eve. "I expect you've muddled up
different things. Until you are used to them, it can be very
difficult to judge whether they approve or disapprove of anything—to judge from their tone, that is. Some Europeans
find them embarrassingly explicit verbalizers, especially the
women. He must have felt very relaxed and at home with
you to talk about the drums at all."

"Oh," said Mrs. Caine. "I didn't realize."

The conversation puttered about for a bit, without ever
regaining the ease and confidence it had possessed earlier on.
They were all three bored, Pibble realized, and both the
women looked drawn and tired. He thanked Mrs. Caine for
his tea and left to interview the old men.

It took two hours and turned out to be almost entirely
wasted time. They all said exactly the same things; they out-
lasted his nerve-racking silences with contemptuous ease;
they remained aloof from his treacherous friendliness and
impervious to his factitious aggression; every question was
considered, then answered with the stately formality of minor
characters in a tragedy by Racine.

Joshua was the most interesting; he was the cook whom

Pibble had nicknamed The Poacher, and his style of conversation was different from the others. Perhaps his vocabulary
was smaller, but he relied less on words than on an elaborate
and expressive code of gestures. He sat on the bed of the
pretty little room which Pibble had collared for his inquisition,
a blob of black flesh, perched like Tenniel's Humpty Dumpty
with tiny legs dangling, while his large, delicate hands fluttered and deprecated, modifying the midnight syllables he
spoke. But all the time his glistening black eyes stared un-
moving at Pibble. If the cook had been a white man, Pibble
realized, it would have been certain that he was frightened
and lying, some old fence who'd had the bad luck to become involved with tearaways who'd taken him deeper in
than even his cupidity cared for, and was now trying to
wheedle his way out of trouble with sighs and grimaces and
a straight, dishonest stare. But how could you tell what moved
behind this alien phiz?

No, he'd slept all night. No, he could think of no reason
for anyone wanting to slay the chief. No, he knew of no
way out of the hut save through the door which Elijah kept.
Yes, he made the *kava*, and had put no more than the usual
number of sleeping tablets in it. Yes, he would have been able
to taste had someone else added more tablets—was he not the
cook? What kind of a cook would he be if he could not
taste a simple thing like that?

A flick of his fingers suggested an abysmal level of efficiency. Pibble shifted his ground.

"Do you think Aaron would have wished to stop the
drumming?" he said.

"Of course." No gesture.

"Did he speak to you about this?"

"No. He did not speak often." A movement of wrists and
elbows, like that of a Thai dancer rejecting a suitor, implied
the aloofness of the chief.

"Why would he wish to stop the drumming?"

"For the sake of the Reverend Mackenzie." The palms were laid together in the attitude of devotion.

"And you didn't feel the same about the Reverend Mackenzie?"

"He bewitched us for a season." A shrug and a spreading of the hands told that witchcraft was the kind of misfortune that might befall anybody. "If he had not come—" A wholly different shrug, saying that anything might have happened.

"But Robert Caine would still have arrived at your village, whether Mr. Mackenzie had been there or not," said Pibble.

Joshua whisked his hands apart and clapped them together, saying, as clear as words, He would have been nothing to us.

"What would you have done?" asked Pibble, curiosity getting the upper hand of duty. "Would you have eaten him?"

"More tales are told than are true," said Joshua, mocking the white man's superstition with a flip of the wrist.

"He'd have been tough," suggested Pibble.

"All adult beasts need care," said Joshua, the glistening stare at last mitigating into professional interest. "A few of the joints might have roast. The hams and the shoulders. With much basting, of course. He was well fleshed, and younger then. Even so, one would need strong herbs to mask that part of the taste which might be rancid. The lesser joints would broil easily enough. The lights—I do not know. I think I would not have used them unless meat were scarce. We had a big lizard in our valley, quick but stupid—hard to catch but easy to trap. Parts of the flesh were succulent, the flavor of a good capon with the texture of crabmeat, but other parts were poisonous. So it might be with a man." The left hand, thrust forward a little, palm up, fingers curled in, commented that all the foregoing was merest supposition and not based on any firsthand knowledge. The eyes regained their intense indifference. Pibble sighed.

"What steps could Aaron have taken to stop the drumming?" he said.

Joshua pouted and put his head on one side. Not a very serious question.

"Well," said Pibble, "what would have happened if he had managed to persuade Dr. Ku that the whole tribe ought to move back to New Guinea?"

Joshua locked his fingers together and folded his thumbs across them, like a prep-school headmaster who finds that he will have to talk to one of the boys about sex a term ahead of schedule. An absorbing but embarrassing point had been raised.

"What would have happened?" he said. "Who can tell?"

Pibble allowed the silence to tick by. The old man stared at him, frightened and motionless, as an exhausted hare crouches in an agony of stillness, ears laid back, corneas bulging—sometimes the beagles miss her, but not often. Pibble, alas, knew his own toothlessness: not for him, now, to raise his head from the grasses, his jowls the color of blackberry jam with the blood of the hare.

"Would you have wanted to go?" he said at last.

Joshua sighed; his shoulders drooped and his hands pattered onto his thighs.

"We are old," he said, "old."

His hands spread out again, in a wide tremulous movement, measuring the distance to New Guinea, and the length the journey had been in years to achieve this new balance of life, and at the same time the shortness of the span left them to discover another conceivable posture.

"But surely," said Pibble, "life in New Guinea would not be so very different from life here. Isn't that the point of all these rituals you keep up? Haven't you begun to return—in spirit, so to speak—by starting this drumming business again?"

"These are not the same drums. The priest does not call the

same spirits. We are not the same men. On the television they told us that when you send back a tame lion to the jungle he can no longer catch meat." His hands made a baffled movement, the spring of a beast that misses.

"You think, then," said Pibble, "that Dr. Ku has served no purpose in keeping all your customs, as far as possible, intact?"

"You are all the same," said Joshua, with an irritable flick of the fingers, "all you people who come in from outside. You all think he has done everything for us, as if we were babies who could do nothing for ourselves. He is nothing—a *parahili*." An effeminate wriggle of arm and shoulder translated the word into the universal language of men. "But he is clever, certainly. He will know that we have changed, even as much as Paul's way of painting has changed."

"Do you like Paul's paintings?" said Pibble. Joshua was the fifth of the old men he had talked to. Ishmael and the two younger ones, Jacob and Daniel, were to come, but he knew that he would get nothing police-like out of any of them. Instead he pursued academic byways—something, after all, might emerge there.

"They are not true paintings." said Joshua. "Not like the ones we have done on our door and in our hut. They are difficult, but they are clever. When I understand them, they make me laugh."

"But the drumming has changed in a way you do understand?"

Joshua nodded solemnly, an affirmative more potent than words.

"And the drumming is important to you?"

Another nod.

"Why?"

"We are dying, policeman. For many hours, for many days, we are dead. But when the drums move in our blood we are alive again for a little. It is like this: an old man has a wife, they were wedded many years past, and even after a feast now he can give her no joy, and his heart says I am old, I am old, soon I will see no more, taste no more, smell no more, and my cousins will bury me. But then his wife gives him leave to take another wife, a young girl with hard muscles, and the old man's strength comes back to him and he has pleasure with her and pleasure with his old wife, too, if he is a good man. So it is with us and the drums. If you could hear them, you might understand." The whole of Joshua's small parable had been accompanied by sensual, obscene, explicit finger play.

"I hope to come tonight," said Pibble.

"The priest will slay the slayer of our chief," said Joshua.

Pibble was jolted back into the path of duty.

"I believe," he said, "that Aaron did intend to move the whole tribe back to New Guinea. If he and Dr. Ku and the women had been agreed on this, could the men's hut have withstood him?"

Joshua's fists bonked together in the head-on collision of opposing stupidities. He gazed mournfully at the smarting knuckles.

"I do not know," he said. "The women have no voice, but the wise man hears them all the time."

Pibble looked at him gloomily. By their own crazy standards, the old men had a motive for killing the chief, and they could have done it, all acting together—drawing lots, presumably, for the actual man who was to wait in ambush. Pibble had been puzzled all along by the question of smell; everyone agreed that Aaron would have been aware of an outsider (Caine, for preference) lurking on the stairs, but in a house that smelled of Kus an extra-strong whiff of Ku might pass unnoticed. Collusion was in the air; all the old men shared the frightened gaze of the hare. But it didn't feel right—Pibble found he trusted the movements of Joshua's hands more than the tongue in anyone's head. Perhaps they were just frightened of authority, dreading the unknown element as a child dreads the jelly it finds in the cavities of cold meat.

Or perhaps one of them—Robin, most likely—had stirred himself to the momentariness of action; he might even have a key, or the knack of moving so softly that the keeper of the door would not be aware of him—after all, they seemed none of them to have heard him stealing out onto the roof through his sliding panel—and now they knew in their hearts that he had done it, but not in their minds. That would account both for the fright and for the apparent truthfulness of all their answers.

In any case, how was Pibble going to prove it? Unless the younger men were more vulnerable, he couldn't see anyone except possibly Robin breaking down, and that not till after months of brainwashing—and pretty *that* would be made to look once the defense learned about it! Fourteen, was he?

Pibble dismissed Joshua, who bowed himself fussily out but immediately beetled back as if he at last had something useful to communicate.

"I believe the best cut," he whispered, "would be slices of the shoulder muscles cut across the grain and beaten very thin. I would fry them with garlic and fennel."

The young men were no more vulnerable, no less frightened—if fright it was. Jacob was voluble, Daniel taciturn, but neither said anything in the least bit useful, beyond confirming that they had heard the old men making bets on how much Pibble would discover in the hut. They were both just as firmly in favor of the drumming as the old men had been, both certain that nothing that had happened in the hut was anyone else's business, least of all Eve's. Pibble had decided to be tough with Jacob, snarling and sneering, but a chance answer betrayed him; the black man hated and distrusted Caine to an irrational extent, he discovered, and after that the interrogation became almost cozy. He found himself wondering whether he would have liked Aaron, aloof and puritan, as much as he liked the lesser members of the tribe. When the last useless silence was over, he walked down the stairs and found his associates Fernham and Strong waiting in the porch.

"Time you went home," he said. "I'm sorry to have kept you. I'll be staying on for a bit. Does that pub do cooked suppers, Strong?"

"Fair to middling, sir."

"If you see Superintendent Graham, will you tell him I'll be down here till about nine? I'm going to listen to a drumming ritual in the men's hut, but it won't get us anywhere, twenty to one. I don't think there's any point in your both coming back tomorrow—if I could have just one chap, you might tell him? I think that's all. Good night."

"Night, sir."

Supper was a misery, stale fish in an ectoplasm sauce, and a lonely silence. When he returned to Flagg Terrace, the door was locked and he had to ring. Rebecca let him in.

"Hello," he said, taking a chilly dip into the interview he had been shirking, "I've been wanting to talk to you. About Robin. Do you know what has been happening upstairs?"

"In the men's hut." The interrogative lilt was beyond her, but she made the question with her eyes.

"Yes," said Pibble.

"Robin . . . drums . . . They have cut . . . his back."

"Yes. How did you know?"

"Robin told me . . . before . . . He said: I will do this . . . I made . . . tears . . . My brother . . . Paka—Paka—Paka—Pakatoluji; he was . . . priest. . . . He lived . . . bitter days. . . . I told . . . Robin. . . . I said you go down a black . . . path; you find . . . at the end. . . . He said . . . do you . . . forbid me. . . . I said: my son . . . you are the . . . nephew of my . . . brother . . . and you are my . . . son."

The large eyes, welling with love amid the puddled face, clamored at him like the eyes of orphans in an Oxfam poster. Sober duty clamored from the other side. Pibble, as usual, compromised.

"I'm not happy about it," he said, "and I shall have to make up my mind what to do. The best thing would be for you and Dr. Ku to go along to the local child-guidance people—I'll send you their address—and consult them. I ought to put in a report about it, but I'll do nothing for a couple of days and give you a chance to make up your mind. Do you understand?"

"I . . . understand. . . . When   you . . . hear . . . the drums, you will understand also."

She stood aside. The blue-white flicker of the TV screen bathed the hall from the S.C.R. Pibble climbed slowly (as Aaron must have climbed the night before) up the carpeted flights to the men's hut. They were all there, waiting for him.

The air was soggy with burned herbs, through whose haze the homemade candles shone yellowly. He could not see right across the room, but the men—all of them except Robin—were squatting in the middle of the floor rolling dice, with clucks and grunts and much thigh-slapping. Pibble hesitated in the doorway until he was noticed.

They rose together, like alarmed pigeons, and one of them, Ishmael, strutted toward him.

"You come at last, policeman," he said. "First we must initiate you; then we can begin. Do not be frightened. In the valley, we had an easy ritual if a stranger from another tribe wished to sit in the men's hut."

"In the valley," rumbled Joshua, "a stranger would have brought a pig."

Pibble winked at him, and the hut swam with the Kus' booming laughter.

"Give me your hand," said Ishmael. "No, palm up."

He held the white hand in his black paw, and quick as a snake-strike the other paw flashed out, a penknife in its fingers, and made a tiny nick on the inside of the wrist. Pibble was too surprised to flinch. Melchizedek stepped forward, drew the drop of blood onto his finger, spat on it, and mixed the liquid into a tiny pile of dust on the floor—a pile which Pibble realized, from the brush marks at its edges, must have been prepared in advance. The old man came up with an index finger covered with the tacky mixture and drew two sweeping curves on Pibble's cheeks, an ephemeral version of the Ku's lifelong facial scars.

"Good," said Ishmael. "Now we can begin. You can sit there, policeman. You need do nothing. You are not a full member of the hut. Tonight the priest will slay the slayer of our chief. Tomorrow you will go to your own place, for justice will have gorged her fill."

Pibble sat in a comfortable nest of rugs at the corner of one of the outer alcoves. From here he could see the whole center of the floor. The men returned to their game and crouched intently as first Daniel and then Joshua made their throws. That, apparently, was the end, for Daniel slapped Elijah jokingly on the shoulder, and Elijah squared up at him like a wrestler. The other Kus laughed and cackled. It was like a group coming out of a pub at closing time. Then, like just such a group, they wavered into the shadows of the alcoves and were gone.

A noise like the pattering of raindrops on a barn roof, endless and formless, coming from nowhere. Imperceptibly the individual patterings gathered themselves into rhythmic shapes; or perhaps it was only the weariness of the ear that turns a clock's tickings at midnight into patterns of emphasis. Now the noise slowed and was obscured by a shuffling, as one of the men writhed backward along the floor. He moved out into the middle of the room, naked, crawling with his hands clasped behind his back and his head only a few inches from the floor. In his teeth, he held a small bag from which dribbled some whitish powder. Slowly he slithered backward, waving his head steadily from side to side as he went. Pibble remembered the rhythmic precision of Paul's practice brush strokes. The man—it was Jacob—was moving in a wide, calculated circle, the dribble of powder from his bag making a precise pattern on the floor. Before he was halfway around, the strain of his posture brought a dew of sweat out all over the blue-black muscles, glistening in the candlelight. A muttering unsyllabled chant joined in with the thud of the drum, then a buzzing whir, and finally an eerie tootling. Jacob cranked his body sideways, nodding jerkily backward and forward to finish his pattern without marring the part which he had already covered, and wriggled back into the dark. The noise, except for the pattering, ceased.

Melchizedek, also naked, walked out of another alcove without ceremony and put a slit-drum into the circle. He did this five times.

The buzzing whir began again, and Ishmael stepped into the circle swinging a bull-roarer. He crouched at the center of the pattern, his left arm apparently motionless above his head, as the scooped wood whanged around above the patterned powder. Then he flicked it out of the air with a crooking of his elbow and walked into the shadows.

A group appeared: four naked men carrying Robin on a loose, swaying litter. The boy's palms fluttered above a small drum which rested on his lap; that was where the pattering came from. They put him in the middle of the circle and left him. He stopped drumming. The overture was finished.

All the men came out into the light, lounging or squatting against the edges of the screens. Robin fidgeted with his drums, adjusting them to suit his convenience. The biggest was a five-foot log which was held clear of the floor at one end by a bipod like a Bren gun's; there were three smaller wooden drums, from one of which he had summoned the raindrop noise, one was made of something unidentifiable, and one looked like a squeezed dustbin. Ishmael swung the bull-roarer loosely from his wrist; Melchizedek had the nose flutes.

Suddenly Robin picked up a tool like an Indian club and beat three rubbing strokes on the biggest drum; it did not boom, but groaned, and the men sighed inward between each stroke. Ishmael started his bull-roarer in a slow, vertical circle which made it emit a deep drone. Robin settled the dustbin drum between his thighs and began to beat it with the heels of his hands in a dull, commonplace rhythm which Pibble recognized as part of the backing to half a hundred pop discs. Melchizedek inserted random poopings from his nose flutes. The bull-roarer droned on, its notes coming in a hypnotic thud as the increased momentum of the down-swing caught it. The men began to bark random syllabic shouts. None of the noises seemed to have anything to do with the others.

Robin fiddled with his rhythm a bit, inserting unnecessary slaps and thumps. The dustbin had a twanging resonance deep inside it, which he was somehow building into a thick continuous note.

"The drums must be warmed before the spirits come."

Joshua had come to squat at Pibble's elbow. His belly, culminating in a protuberant navel, sagged outward and down toward his knees. The whole mass trembled slightly, a continuous excited shiver. The note of the rhythm changed; Robin was working steadily now with three drums, the two wooden ones making a flat, dead noise under his left hand while his right hand kept the metal one alive. This he was working now to a slower and slower beat, catching its internal resonance just as it died away into whimperings. At first he filled the gaps with a hiccupping rattle on the small drums; then he added to this a backhanded slap at the long log which groaned its deep note against the metal whanging of the dustbin. Pibble thought he had some sort of wooden knuckle-duster laced to the back of his hand, but it was hard to see through the dust and smoke.

Jacob stalked out from the wings and began to strut in front of the circle, as clockwork in motion as the springtime pigeons Pibble had watched that morning. One of the old men handed him a bottle, which he tilted back and drank from. The bull-roarer had stopped, but the old men were calling excitedly together, still in monosyllables, backing the compulsive iteration of the drums. Jacob kept the bottle and continued his strutting. Suddenly he staggered in his march, hunched his shoulders together, threw his head back, and began to glide around the room in a wallowing lope. From his mouth came a high, absurd voice, the voice of a don on "The Critics," speaking the Ku language in rapid spasms. He tilted the bottle back again, but this time most of the liquid spilled down into his beard and over his neck and shoulders. He gulped unheeding.

"Good," said Joshua. "It is Korapu. He is drunk and a bully and a coward, but he comes before."

"Before the green snake?" whispered Pibble.

"Do not name it!" whispered Joshua. "It is ill fortune!"

He moved away from Pibble, as if from the contamination of cholera. The beat of the drums was now very loud. The whole room seemed to have acquired the internal resonance of the metal drum, so that the boards and beams picked up harmonics from each thud and rattle and groan and transmitted them along the framework of Pibble's skeleton. Robin was sitting on the far edge of the light, his whole body slippery with sweat as he worked his instruments into the lurches of the coward god's dance. Korapu broke from the figure of eight through which he had been reeling and rushed straight at Pibble. Pibble rose in self-defense. Korapu screamed a cackling curse and thrust his bottle under Pibble's nose. Pibble took it, put it to his lips, tilted it back, and sucked. Christ! It was raw spirit! He choked halfway through his swallow, did the nose trick with the reeking acid, choked again, and shook his head, his ears singing. Korapu cackled again, a zany's laugh this time, and reeled away. Pibble sat down.

Several times more, Korapu left his dance to share a drink with the watchers; they humored him and took their swigs and, when the bottle was empty, gave him another one. The second time he came to Pibble, Pibble managed the encounter with more dignity, answering the jeering babble with the only Latin he could remember, *"Bis dat qui cito dat,"* and swallowing his tot with a full command over his gullet. The old men were getting bored with this minor demon and beginning to whisper among themselves when Robin caught him in mid-stagger with three strokes at the long log which cut the ribald ecstasies of sound. Korapu fled. The black body he had ridden shriveled and collapsed. Jacob knelt in the middle of the floor in the attitude of the embryo, his torso pulsing like that of an embryo as he gulped, exhausted, at the smoky air. The men didn't seem to look at him.

Robin settled into a slow movement, rubbing a heavy throb out of the long log and counterpointing it with a subdued tapping at one of the small drums. It was a sullen, earthy noise, too slow for any human rhythm, going on and on, subduing thought. The men stood still and waited. Ishmael started his bull-roarer again, timing the emphasis of its down-swing to underpin the groanings of the big drum. There were no shouts now. After ages of sound, Robin added a fluttering double beat to the pattern, and then another. The lump of black flesh in the middle of the floor stopped its heaving and began to twitch. A new life flowed into it, slow and cold. It stirred upward, jointless. The head of the man it inhabited craned forward, his eyeballs showed only white, his tongue stuck out between stretched lips. A whispering hiss came from the roof beams.

All the men shouted together, and the hiss answered them. The drums boomed on, busy with innumerable interlocking rhythms. Melchizedek made a short speech in the Ku language and the hiss replied. It was just a hiss, with no syllables in it. Melchizedek spoke again, with the emphasis of a man arguing a case, but before he had finished the hiss cut him short. The men began to sing all together, a chant of short sentences each slightly varied from the last. In the middle of one of these sentences, the snake god left; there was a quick, agonizing spasm and Jacob bowed forward from the hips, his head nearly banging the floor. Then he stood up, scratched his ribs and neck, walked over to where Korapu's bottle stood, took a long swig, and sat down next to Ishmael.

After that, Daniel did a clowning obscene dance in his own person. No spirit came to ride him, and the men shouted happily at him as he bounced and postured. Robin played trickily with the drums but without intensity. When Daniel was tired, he sat down and the men carried Robin out of the circle. The cuts in his back looked raw and nasty. Pibble wondered whether they'd had the sense to use antiseptic on them.

Elijah wobbled affably over.

"Now we will drink *kava* and sleep," he said. "Would you like some?"

"No, thank you," said Pibble. "I must stay awake tonight. That was very interesting. What on earth was in the bottle?"

Elijah winked and brought the key from the bag which now hung flopping on his chest.

"You must show us round Scotland Yard someday," he said. "That would also be interesting. Good night."

"Good night," said Pibble, and went groggily down the stairs. He recognized that he was in a state of half shock—vaguely the same sort of walking-dead feeling as he'd had when Richard Foyle, his first boss and only hero, had been convicted of corruption. More than vaguely; once again the intellectually stimulating and cheerful surface of his job had suddenly rotted away, leaving only the wicked skeleton. He was sure now that the drumming ritual was wicked, a corruption of humanity as horrid, in its way, as Richard's involvement with the Smith machine had been.

Light glared out from the door of Eve's living room. A voice said, "That you, Jimmy?" so Pibble went in. Paul was lying on the floor reading *Graphis*, and Eve and Ned Rickard sat together on the sofa, solemnly regarding an elaborate structure of string which Eve held on her fingers.

"The next bit is not easy," said Eve in her don's voice, "and is considered as a *pons asinorum*, or shibboleth, among the tribes of the Ku group. The tribes on the other side of the big range, as well as those in the coastal strip and most of the islands, have a completely different cultural history which includes a form of cat's cradle a man can play by himself. Indeed, this is perhaps the most discriminating criterion of the cultural origins of a tribe, as it is completely independent of any oral tradition or communication. You have to be shown. A man from one of the other groups of tribes might have picked up the earlier stages, but unless he had learned and practiced this one among the other children in his village he would probably make a mess of it. Do you think you can get this onto your own hands, Superintendent, and I will show you?"

"I don't see any way in," said Ned. "Try and tell me. It doesn't matter if I make a mess of it, as I ought to have a chat with Jimmy. I hope he's been treating you proper."

"He would have made a sound scholar," said Eve seriously.

Paul looked up from his magazine with a booming chuckle, waved a paw at Pibble, and returned to the study of a group of André François's posters.

"Now, Superintendent," said Eve, "you have two problems. First, as you can see, the initial asymmetry involved in the crossing of strings in any cat's cradle pattern has now multiplied itself to a point where we must either go back, or tangle ourselves in a knot, or evolve a countervalent asymmetry. The left hand is quite easy. Put your index and thumb round the upper crossing and hook your little finger round the inside of the lowest string. You are going to have to turn that hand inward and down when the time comes. Now, with your right hand, take the lower crossing between the little finger and the ball of the right thumb; that's right. Move your wrist out a bit. You are going to have to turn that hand inward and up. Tuck your two middle fingers out of the way. The problem is to put your thumb and index into the two loops that will be made by the slackening of the upper crossing after they have traversed the first parallel string and before they come to the second."

"I see what you mean about oral communication," said Ned. "Are you ready? One, two, three, go!"

The four hands danced together in a quick flight. One of them stumbled. Ned cursed and then laughed, gazing at the meaningless mess of string on his hands.

"Not bad," said Eve. "You did catch one, Superintendent. If you had caught them both, I would have owed you a suckling pig. What happened upstairs, Mr. Pibble? I would be most grateful if you let me have some notes when you have finished with the criminal aspects of this affair."

"Hell, Jimmy," said Ned. "What've you been up to? You look as if you'd been walking the fells with ghouls."

"I have," said Pibble. "You look better, Ned. Has something broken?"

"Not half. Come outside and I'll tell you—it's your doing, really. Scuse us, Dr. Ku."

"Good night," said Pibble. "I'll be back about nine in the morning. Perhaps I'll have some ideas by then. In any case, there are several things I ought to talk to you about, I suppose."

"Good night," said Eve and Paul together.

It was quite dark in the street. Only the lamp at the end was working. Ned walked over to a long car, whose body-work gleamed glossy in the faint illumination, and rested an arm across it in an ownerly way.

"Like my new bus?" he said. "The Ass. Com. ordered me to take it. It's the bulletproof job."

"Crippen, Ned, are you as near as that?"

The car was a souped-up Mercedes saloon, both joke and myth at the Yard, the folly of a long-retired Commissioner who had convinced himself that Chicago was coming to London any month now. It would do a hundred and forty; its bodywork was solider than most chassis; the interior was pitted with pockets for small arms, tear-gas cylinders, smoke bombs, and such; there was a searchlight on the roof as well as the usual loudspeaker. Pibble leaned over the roof to feel for its controls.

"It's got a trigger grip inside," said Ned. "You can switch it on and off, turn it, and tilt it all with one hand. I say, Jim, that flat is going to be a breakthrough. We knew it existed but we didn't know that it mattered. I've had five chaps worrying at it all afternoon, and we've turned up trumps. It's registered in Mrs. Furlough's maiden name—she's a nice lass, Roedean, breeds West Highlands down at Sonning, thinks her hubby's in show business—and Burnaby did a fluke with the carrot merchant opposite—it's just off Covent Garden, you know—who remembered the name of the builders who did the alterations last summer, because he was thinking of putting on an extra bathroom himself and was on the lookout for builders. I suppose the breaks always come in the end if you wait for them. You know one of the things they put in where any normal man would have put a hanging cupboard? A ruddy great fireproof, thiefproof steel filing cabinet. We're going in tonight, and I'm due for the sack if it's got nothing in it except theatre programs. Furlough's got some biggish friends."

"Good luck," said Pibble. "Will you be able to keep Miss Hermitage out of it?"

"Hope so, Jim. She's a dish, isn't she, our Nan?"

"What about Caine?"

"Our legal Johnnies don't think he's broken the law," said Ned flatly. "Besides, I don't want him in in case the whole show gets mucked up with accusations of personal bias. Besides, Sukie seems happy with him. How's your show going?"

"Getting nowhere," said Pibble tiredly. The shock of the drumming ritual and that abominable liquor seemed to have drained him of will. He looked up at the crenelations of Flagg Terrace, where the façade stood black against the reflected blue-pink glare of neon which is all London ever seems to know of night. Robin was presumably up there somewhere, mooning on the roof and becoming a schoolboy again. Pibble stared at the pitch-black vertical shadows that hung where the beams of the single street lamp could not reach to the brickwork. You'd never see a climber working his way across there, even if you were looking. Yes, you would, though! At least you'd see *something*.

Pibble opened the near door quietly and slid on his back across the front seats till he could look out of the far window. The movement in the shadow seemed to have gone, but he knew where it ought to be, and reached up for the pistol grip of the searchlight. Lying like this, he had to work it with his hand back to front, but he aimed it roughly and tilted it back and switched on.

Missed! A circle of brickwork and pipes and window ledge glared into being too low and to the left. He steadied the searchlight up and caught the climber five feet below the battlements.

Dear God, the climber was moving quickly, like a scurrying spider. He was too small! He was making a mess of it!

Struck by the solid blaze like a rioter caught in a power hose, the climber staggered in his lissome movements. A straining white face shone for a moment over his shoulder; then the right hand, no longer guided by the light-blinded eyes, grabbed an inch below the overflow pipe it was reaching for while the left hand had already let go of a drip course. The body, face still twisted to the fatal summons of the searchlight, heeled slowly back from the wall, feet splayed along an inch-wide slope of bath waste, then peeled away and plunged outside the circle. It fell four stories into the basement area, but there was no cry. Only a thud like a sack of cement dropped too heavily onto a path and bursting a little at the corners.

Pibble weaseled out of the car and ran across the road. Ned was already there, craning over the railings. Pibble craned beside him and looked down to where the body lay broken-backed on the spikes of the cross-railings between the areas of No. 8 and No. 9. The light was on in the women's kitchen, so that you could see at once that the climber was dead, not even twitching, with a mess of blood black below the body. You could see the off-mouse hair trailing downward. You could see who it was.

"Oh God!" said Pibble, "she was left-handed!"

He moved his hand along the railing toward Ned and touched something loose, a pair of National Health spectacles, both the strong lenses shattered. Instinctively he held the frame out consolingly to Ned.

"Crippen," he said, "I'm—"

He never saw Ned's fist that came looping out of the dark, but felt the stunning agony in his nose and all over his face, and the helpless backward reeling, and then . . .

HAMMERSMITH HOSPITAL
150 Du Cane Road, W. 12

Casualty Department

NAME OF PATIENT: Pibble, James   AGE: 53 (?)

ADDRESS: c/o New Scotland Yard   OCCUPATION: POLICE

29/5/67 10 P.M.	Brought in by police car. Injured in street brawl. Unable to give a history. According to driver of police car, was struck on nose and fell back against step.	T = 98.3 P = 60/m BP = 125/90

O/E   *Injuries*   1. Bloody nose, obviously   R = 20

                            broken

                 2. 1½" cut on back of

                            head behind R. ear

                 3. Abrasion R. elbow

CNS: Drowsy, rambling, uncooperative

        but responds to painful stimuli

        Pupils reg: react to L & A

        Fundi: NAD

        Cranial Nn: No obvious lesions,

                            difficult to test be-

                            cause of lack of co-

                            operation.

        Limbs: Tone:

	R	L
Upper	+	+
Lower	+	+

Motor: Power and coordination
not tested due to lack of
cooperation.

Reflexes:

	R	L
TJ	+	+
BJ	+	+
JJ	+	+
KJ	+	+
AJ	+	+
Plantars	↓	↓
Abdo:	$\frac{V}{V}$	$\frac{V}{V}$

Sensory: Pain

Touch
Temp., etc. ⎫ Not tested
Vibration ⎭

General Examn: Pulse 60, good vol
BP 125/95

CVS HS I & II none
added

RS Trachea central
Expansion
good =

PN resonant

BS vesic, none
added

Abdo: Soft, no tenderness or
guarding
LKS not felt, no masses.
Gutsounds

△ Concussed #? skull

℞ Suture of scalp wound, then for
skull X-ray & admit to ward for
routine observation. Get ENT
surgeon to see.

Skull X ray: fissured # across base of
skull not extending to
vault.

The trouble with delirium is this—that the trouble with delirium is this—that the trouble with delirium is that unless you get a hold on yourself man and keep a hold on yourself and keep keeping a hold on yourself and—unless—and—you—unless—and you just fall backward and backward and backward into a nasty mucky messy drivelogue going round and round and round and a handsome male head with bruise sacs under the eyes going round and round and round in the cannibal pot and it'll never be cooked laughing at you like that because it married a left-handed wife who chops up her left thumb slowly, slowly as though it were vital that every strip should be the same precise width because she doesn't want you to see that if she were chopping up her *right* thumb with her left hand she'd be able to go snip snap snop and it'd all be done in a second and you'd be able to plaster it up with knots of string wound in and out like the cultural traditions on the other side of the mountain of love and never mind about the meaty smell because it's been in your nostrils all night and you can't expect to smell it in the morning any more than an old man who's been with a lady all evening can be expected to smell her waiting to murder him with a piece of wood or a stone picked up by the path and you can't expect—and you can't expect—and you can't—get a hold on yourself man and keep a hold on yourself and keep keeping a hold—get a *hold*—expect a secretive old man but very honorable too not to come waddling round in his pajamas to tell his lady friend that he was stopping his installments on the sacrifice—twenty years of little outgoings after the first down payment and in the end it had not turned out to have been worth while—and so she knew—she knew—and we knew she knew because she made a mess about the drums which he *had* talked about—of course he had because he was an honorable man and he'd tell her the reason and show her the penny too—but she'd made a mess about the drums—and the

drums had made a mess of her when the snake god killed her
mashed her into bleeding pulp which was what Ned wanted
to do with Furlough and perhaps she'd known about Furlough too—more than Bob realized Miss Hermitage had said
and you'll never see her again with her gawky walk—she looks
different already and tells her real name to her clients before
she's got a stocking off and she'll kill herself next Christmas
with a college scarf round her neck because she was a truth
addict—but Mrs. Caine would lie Ned said and go up to the
police station pretending to have lost keys and asking about
a missing husband—so she hadn't known about Furlough
then—but perhaps she took steps to find out and then she'd
know like she'd known what Aaron had stolen only she
stopped herself saying it and like she'd known that Caine—
was a mover-on and that was the foundation of a happy
marriage believe it or not but the foundations were sand and
when Bob got turfed out he'd leave her of course Miss
Hermitage had said but she was a sharp princess who wanted
to stay with her loathsome worm and if I want something
I want it—and—if I want somebody dead I want him dead
and while he's walking home I go and pick up a shiny *piton*
from my husband's desk and then I remember about the owl
so I put it back in the wrong place and go and bash my old
pal all for the sake of a pair of bruise-colored sacs going
round and round with bits and bobs of people's behavior
swirling past in the stew—bits of Bob and parts of the flesh
are succulent but other parts are poisonous—and the eyes
laugh because Bob was the catalyst and when the explosion
is over all that's left of God's chemistry set is Bob untouched
and laughing because he lured you into believing he'd do
anything for himself when he could get someone else to do
it and our legal Johnnies don't think he's broken the law and
the law is above our customs but there may be matters you
do not understand any more than you can see the fish in the

stomach of a heron any more than you can understand why a cuddly admiral's daughter the daughter of a cuddly admiral the cuddly daughter of an admiral any more than you can understand why why why why got it! "They that mock at Paradise woo at Cora Lynn" because it's Australian and her dad reads her Wodehouse now she's a big girl but he read her Kipling when she was younger and children are easily bored even by prolonged excitement so it would be a kindness to take the body away a kindness to take the tiresome old puritan out of the permissive system which he was irritating after all Our Father was very averse to overriding anyone unlike some I could name who want a jungle to tidy and are in and out of the jungle whenever there's scarlet fever because they're nurses and Ned had said she was between hospitals and her voice had the sharp reasonableness no not of a businesswoman in a B film but a sister telling Gregory Peck to stay in bed and so they know exactly where to hit and exactly where to find a loose owl because they're in and out of the jungle whenever there's scarlet fever and the jungle's where they live their strong cruel tiger life and they're too stupid to see that this is something different and their agent will chalk it up against the future because he's that sort and he's more important than our irrelevant little tragedy here the breaks always come in the end you fish but it has its moments when you see a slight change in the surface and color of the water and you know there's a big one there and the question is can you get him out but who'll be a farthing worse off if we never find out what happened here so vey wouldn't send one of ver big boys out on a kinky little case like vis too much to lose nuffing to gain they'd send Pibble because it's your cup of tea honest send honest Pibble honest Iago Pibble to nose around like a maggot in the glass-sided ants' nest with his scholarly inquisitiveness and oh my

lord beware of jealousy it will send you beagling after a
white Othello with bruise sacs under his eyes and the hell
with the black one who's already reached the butt and very
seamark of his utmost sail and it's you who'll be the catalyst
while the head goes laughing round in we call it stew you
who'll tell her that Robin says he could name the murderer
if he chose and you who'll lie on your back and fiddle with
the trigger grip and make a blind guess too low and to the
left blinded by the obvious blinded by a searchlight blinded
too blinded to notice ah no you noticed there was something
clumsy about the way she was sewing but you'd put the
plaster onto her curving thumb that very morning onto her
curving thumb with its nail bitten to the quick her left thumb
her perfect woman slips sensation curving left thumb because
she'd been wrestling with her right hand to open the tin not
her left hand which she would have managed easily but her
right not her left right left right get a *hold* on yourself man if
I haven't said that before get a hold he said and so she got
a hold and she used her thumb with the plaster to hold the
needle and you saw it her left thumb to hold the needle hold
the needle hold the needle but it's stuck in the groove and goes
round and round like the laughing head in the stew saying
hold the needle hold the needle hold the needle.

"Mike," the nurse said, "will you be coming up this way
soon? I'm in Prince Albert."

"Anything for you, Mary, darlint. Whassamatter?"

"Nothing much, but I've a concussion who's a bit more
restless than he ought to be. He's keeping some of the others
awake."

"Arrah, I wouldn't be minding keeping you awake one of
these nights, darlint."

"I detest stage Irishmen."

"I'll go to plastic surgery tomorrow and have me freckles removed. In the meantime, I'll come up and give your joker a jab."

Oblivion is not to be hired, but they can give it to you with a needle, with a needle, with a needle.

Pibble woke late, by hospital standards. His nose felt like a wet sandbag and his head sang with pain. He was still drinking his Codis when Superintendent Graham rolled in, wearing a suit which looked as though he'd put on half a stone since he'd worn it last. He was carrying a brown paper bag.

"Hello, Sandy," said Pibble. Both his nostrils were blocked with blood and his voice came very guttural.

"Morning, Jimmy. I've brought you some tangerines. Grapes are Ass. Com.'s and above."

"Thanks, Sandy. I've made a fair old mess of things, I'm afraid."

"D'you want me to hold the fort on the Kus, or shall I ask for someone else from the Yard?"

"No point. Mrs. Caine killed him but there's no proving it. The only thing you can do to ease my conscience is to get a doctor to look at Robin's back—he's one of the children. Have a word with Dr. Ku first."

"Right you are, Jimmy. What happened to you?"

"Didn't Ned Rickard tell you?"

"Rickard's dead."

"Dead!"

"Aye. He dumped you here and rushed off to raid a flat in Soho; at least that's what I hear. There were villains there, burning papers and carting others away, and a couple of them had shotguns. Rickard stopped a load of buckshot with his stomach. They've got about five hundred men down there now, but they aren't in yet, last I heard. Burnaby rang to say this Caine was somehow involved, and he thought Rickard might have said something useful to you."

"No, I don't think so. Christ, Sandy!"

"Nurse said I wasn't to excite you, as they want you out by this afternoon, so I've left all the papers outside. What hit you?"

"Ned did. Mrs. Caine had just fallen off the building and he started pointing up at something when I walked into his gesture. Then I suppose I fell back and cracked my skull on something. Does my wife know?"

"Hospital rang her last night. What was Mrs. Caine doing on the building?"

"Climbing across to murder Robin. I'd told her he said he knew who'd killed the old man, and I'd told her he'd be out on the roof. I put her up there, Mac, and then I pulled her off with that bloody searchlight."

"Easy, Jimmy, easy. She was a villain, too."

"Yeah, I suppose so."

"Why'd she do it? Was she a nut?"

"Not really. She was obsessed with Caine. She loved him, Sandy, probably more than you or I will ever love anyone, villain and all. She sat at home and bit her fingernails down to the quick for him. I think she knew about Furlough—"

"Burnaby said something about that," interrupted Graham. "He said he became so worried about Rickard a few months ago that he sent Mrs. Caine an anonymous letter, telling her all about her husband. Does that make sense?"

"Yes. But don't pass it on, Sandy. Ah well. Anyway, she persuaded herself that Aaron Ku could get Dr. Ku to turn Caine out of his flat."

"That doesn't sound much of a motive to me."

"Miss Hermitage told me that if he was turned out he would leave Mrs. Caine, too. He'd apparently done something like that before. And Mrs. Caine said something, I've forgotten what—I remembered it last night. . . . Oh God . . ."

"Take it easy, Jim. Take it easy. The only point is that you're sure she killed the other one?"

"Pretty well. What was she doing climbing across in the dark if she wasn't on her way to kill Robin? And pretending to be right-handed whenever there was a policeman in the room! Dear Lord, I was slow! How're you getting on with your sex maniac, Sandy?"

"Not a sausage. I ought to be getting back to him now. But first you'd best tell me, in simple words which a poor Celt can understand, just what did happen, and what you think happened. I'll have to put a bod on it to tidy up the messes you've left."

"Ah, hell, I suppose so. Dr. Ku brought the remains of the tribe back from New Guinea. She'd inherited enough money from her mother to allow them to set up as a tribe on their own, keeping their own customs. She owns all Flagg Terrace, you know."

"Does she, now?" said Graham. "That must be worth a pretty penny."

"Yes. That's what caused the trouble. It's worth enough to take them back to New Guinea and set up again in a valley— to go native, you might say."

"Why'd they want to do that?"

"Aaron wanted to—the one who was murdered. The old men had become bored, and were turning back to a rather nasty but exciting kind of paganism, but Aaron was an ardent Christian. He thought he'd be able to bring them to their senses on their own ground. He didn't know that Eve—Dr. Ku, that is—wouldn't have let them go, because she wanted to stay in London for the sake of Paul's painting. But Aaron warned Mrs. Caine about what he was trying to do (*he* thought Eve was staying for the sake of Caine), and then *she* thought that'd mean the Caines' being turned out of their rent-free basement and Caine leaving her. So she climbed across and bashed him—she'd been a nurse, and knew how. You ought to be able to find marks of her movements on the pipes, if you can get some ladders up before it rains—she wasn't wearing gloves."

"Right. Damned expensive ideas you have, Jimmy." Graham pulled out a pad from a strained pocket and made a note.

"Sorry. That's what the two-headed penny was about. Caine had used it to trick the tribe into letting him stay with them, and Aaron thought it'd be the clincher for making Eve get rid of him. I daresay Caine would tell you about it now if you twisted his arm a bit. Miss Hermitage said he was as soft as butter."

"He's gone," said Graham. "There's nothing anyone can lay on him, as far as I can see, but he's run. There's a call out, but you can't tell how long it'll be."

"Yes," said Pibble. "She said he'd do that."

"Who? Mrs. Caine?"

"Nan Hermitage. How are the others taking it, Sandy?"

"Not been down there myself, but Fernham rang up to say they were having a community hymn singing; all the gloomy ones—'Abide with Me,' and so on. He said they were quiet, but the men looked sulky. That all, Jimmy?"

"I've blotted my copybook with this one, Sandy. Heard what they think about it at the Yard?"

"Don't you worry, Jimmy boy. They're all too busy running round in circles after Furlough. They won't notice a slight cockup over a silly little case like this."

"I suppose not."

"Anything else I can do for you?"

"Be a pal and find out if anything's been done for Ned's mother. She's a little old saint, stone blind."

"Right. Crewe sent you a letter. Bye, then."

There was a handwritten note, saying, "This is from my girl in traffic control. I got quite pally with the chap I saw at London University, and the feeling seems to be that Dr. Ku is unique in a very specialized and very limited field, and that her ideas—as distinct from her knowledge—are on the old-fashioned side. Chaos here. Get well soon."

"This" was a typewritten flimsy, which said:

EPHRAIM FLAGG, 18??–1893, born in Newcastle. Nothing else known of his early life. Appeared in London in the mid-sixties with a small sum of capital and set up as a builder, at a time when London was expanding uncontrollably with the advent of the suburban railways. Flagg soon became notorious as a jerry-builder even in a jerry-building age. His property speculations were accompanied by lavish corruption of officials. He was never successfully sued, but only just escaped the attentions of a Parliamentary Commission—it was alleged by spending a fortune in bribes. In 1885, Flagg was converted to a sect of ultraenthusiastic evangelists whose moving spirit was the Reverend Richard Oakenhouse (later convicted for a series of frauds on elderly widows) and who called themselves the Pure People. Flagg wished to use part of his fortune to build them a church, but worship inside buildings was contrary to their tenets. However, Oakenhouse persuaded him to atone for his previous sins by building a terrace of perfect houses for the Pure People to inhabit. Oakenhouse vetted every contractor before he would pass them as workers worthy of their task. It was only when the buildings were almost completed that Flagg discovered how much commission Oakenhouse had squeezed out of the contractors. In his rage, he left the Pure People and named the Terrace after himself. The Minister has recently refused to place a preservation order on Flagg Terrace.